LOVE HIM HATE HIM

Chris Bedell

Between the Lines PUBLISHING

"An Indie for Indies"

LOVE HIM
HATE HIM

Cover Design by Suzanne Johnson

Willow River Press
Between the Lines Publishing
410 Caribou Trail
Lutsen, MN 55612
btwnthelines.com

First Published: February 2021

Willow River Press is an imprint of Between the Lines Publishing. The Liminal Books name and logo are trademarks of Between the Lines Publishing.

The publisher is not responsible for websites (or their content) that are not owned by the publisher.

ISBN: 978-1-950502-35-6 (paperback)
Printed in the United States

CHAPTER 1

Evelyn Sinclair was everywhere and nowhere.

Like when I was chatting with her by her locker one second, and the next she'd disappeared. Or when Evelyn made a cryptic remark and the comment stayed with me longer than it should've. Or when I sat in the backseat of Gavin's car. I was next to my friend, Natalie, and Gavin was driving while Mona sat beside him in the passenger seat. Evelyn wasn't in the car, yet her name had come up a dozen times in the last five minutes.

I sighed. "Ending our friendship with Evelyn seems extreme."

Gavin took his eyes off the road for a beat. "Easy for you to say, Connor. You're the only one Evelyn hasn't hurt."

"How'd you feel if you were Natalie, and Evelyn had outed *your* secret crush to the whole school?" Mona asked.

My shoulders tensed. "Wouldn't happen. I don't like anyone."

Mona scoffed. "I've seen the intense eye contact between you and Liam. Can't make that up."

Sweat clung to my brow. Mona was too close to the truth. If I wasn't careful, then she might figure out about last spring.

"What are you saying?" I asked.

"Nothing." Mona unzipped her purse, then grabbed her lipstick and coated her lips with a bright shade of purple.

I loosened my seatbelt. "Outing the crush was cruel, but why ditch Evelyn now? It isn't like she hasn't made mistakes before. Like snitching to Gavin's lacrosse coach about his steroids, or ratting out Mona to her English teacher last spring…"

"You're proving my point," Mona interrupted. "Have you forgotten what happened after Evelyn tattled about my plagiarism?"

I bit my lip. "I'm sure failing English and attending summer school couldn't have been easy…"

"No shit," Mona said. "Try being grounded the summer before your junior year of high school."

"But Evelyn wasn't lying—you plagiarized your English essay," I pointed out.

Mona threw a glance at me, her glare accentuating her menacing green eyes. "Whose side are you on?"

I was right, though. If Evelyn was beyond redemption, then she wouldn't have cared about honesty.

Gavin honked at the driver in front of us, then turned left and barreled down a new street. "I don't know what you see in Evelyn, man."

"Someone doing one bad thing doesn't mean they're evil," I said.

"Maybe in fiction," Mona said.

Gavin grunted after the traffic light turned green. "You didn't answer my question. I wanna know why you bother with Evelyn."

I wiped my palms on my shorts. "She was the first person who accepted my bisexuality. It gave me the confidence to come out."

"That doesn't change the fact that Evelyn is an awful person," Gavin said. "Plus, eighth grade was a long time ago."

"We could've finished our food before leaving," I changed the subject. "Kind of wasteful."

"Only you'd think about food right now," Mona muttered.

"A twenty-minute delay wouldn't have mattered," I replied, resisting the urge to raise my voice. As much as I hated admitting the truth, Mona was probably right. Food was the least of our concerns, even though it really did matter to me. I was a foodie – there was just nothing more comforting than a good meal.

"I'm more interested in Mona's comment about Liam." Gavin paused at a stop sign before making a right turn and driving down a new road.

"Maybe you should leave it alone," Mona said.

"Connor was squirming," Gavin chimed in.

"If you've got something to say, then say it," I said.

"Are you hoping being friends with Evelyn will give you an in with Liam since he's her twin brother?" Gavin asked.

I shook my head several times. "Liam isn't gay or bi."

"He's never had a girlfriend, let alone bragged about a crush," Gavin pointed out.

"So?" I asked.

Gavin looked at me for a fleeting second. "The other guys on the lacrosse team and football team have."

"Lots of people are single in high school," I said.

"Single, yes—celibate, not so much," Gavin countered. "And then there's Liam's constant need to spout homophobic shit."

My stomach lurched. It was impossible to fathom that what Gavin was implying was actually true. But if Liam had never made a racy comment about a girl and was constantly making homophobic comments, then there really was only one logical conclusion. I wouldn't speak the conclusion into existence, though—I couldn't. Not after what had transpired with Liam, because that secret would die with me. Secrecy was just simpler. This way, I couldn't get my feelings hurt again.

I snorted. "You haven't made your point."

"Forget it," Gavin said.

I sniggered. "Have you forgotten I hate Liam?"

Mona giggled. "You never told us what went on between you two."

"That's my prerogative," I said.

I wrinkled my nose. "Have it your way."

Natalie leaned into my right ear. "Everything okay?"

I dug my nails into my palms, almost drawing blood. Didn't matter if Natalie hadn't meant anything by her comment. Fleeting guilt overcame me—she was displaying more politeness for me than I had for her. I should've been more furious with Evelyn for outing Natalie's crush to the entire school. But I couldn't eliminate Evelyn from my life. Not yet, at least. Doing so seemed unfair. Youthful indiscretions—like the unkind things Evelyn had done—happened to most people. Whether people accepted the truth or not, a lot of people did stuff they weren't proud of when they were kids or teenagers—stuff they'd just have to live with.

"Yes," I forced out. "Anyway, there's something you haven't considered yet. Being pissed at Evelyn is one thing, but don't forget about all the good stuff she's done. Have you forgotten all the parties we've attended because of her?"

"Not our fault if you're lonely," Gavin said.

Mona gave Gavin a dirty look but didn't speak.

"Sorry." Gavin shifted in his seat. "Shouldn't have said that."

I ran my fingers through my gel-slicked hair. "Doesn't matter. But… I mean, have you guys ever considered there might be an explanation for the questionable things Evelyn does?"

Most people might not have bothered defending Evelyn to Gavin, Mona, and Natalie, but I tried. This way, I knew I was doing everything I could.

"Really gonna play the dead mommy card?" Mona asked. "Evelyn's gotta become an adult at some point."

"Losing a parent early in life isn't fun," I said.

"And we're sorry your father died, but a parent's death doesn't excuse shitty behavior," Gavin said.

I whipped my head back and forth. "I never said it did; just trying to give context."

Gavin coughed. "More like enabling."

I pressed my head against the car window while a gust of wind pushed a pile of red, orange, and yellow leaves down the road. It was hard to believe it was already the second week of September. Some trite ideas were true no matter how corny they sounded, like that time moved faster than anticipated.

Time. There was something nobody ever had enough of. Like my father. My life had just been beginning when he passed. And I couldn't help thinking about all this time I wouldn't have with my dad. More specifically, the memories he wouldn't share with me. Like prom. Or high school graduation. Or college graduation. Or me starting a career.

"Let's not fight." Natalie flipped her auburn hair over her shoulders. "Evelyn would want that."

"I still can't get over her name," Mona said. "What kind of parent names their kid Evelyn? It's like something from the 1930s."

"Are you kidding?" I asked.

Mona shrugged. "It was an honest question."

"You can keep being Evelyn's friend if you want," Gavin returned to the original topic. "But if you do, you can't be our friend."

"That's harsh," Natalie piped up.

Thank goodness for Natalie. If I was right, she had a future as a diplomat. Most people wouldn't have bothered to show the level-headedness she did.

"Natalie has a point," Mona said. "He can be friends with Evelyn— he just can't discuss her in front of us. What would we ever do without Connor's insightful commentary?"

"Whatever," Gavin muttered.

"What about the football team now and the lacrosse team in the spring?" I asked. "Liam might mention Evelyn at some point."

"And I'll deal with it when he does," Gavin said.

"Evelyn might be a lot of things, but she isn't stupid. There's no way she's gonna be surprised by this conversation," Mona said.

"What do you mean?" I asked.

Mona remained silent for a beat. "She got a 4.0 GPA last year."

I bit my lip, stopping myself from laughing—sensitivity was necessary if I didn't wanna start more trouble. "Admit it—you're jealous of her."

Mona grimaced. "Duh. Why else do you think she'd betray Gavin and me? She wanted Gavin for herself."

"I'm thankful the coach just benched me for the last couple games of the season; could've been a lot worse." Gavin made a left turn, then sped faster when the car behind us kept tailgating.

"Feel like us not calling or texting first is odd, though," Mona said.

I sniffed. Little late for Mona to express doubt after joining with Gavin to crucify me for empathizing with Evelyn.

"Better this way," Natalie said. "She won't see it coming."

The clunky sound of Gavin's ignition halted after he parked by the curb of Evelyn's house.

We undid our seatbelts and got out.

Except I—like Mona, Natalie, and Gavin—didn't bother trekking up Evelyn's driveway. A person sporting a paramedic jacket was pushing a stretcher toward an ambulance. I made a fist as the paramedic glanced down at the body bag, only to shake his head. The bag was partially opened, revealing a portion of the occupant's head. It was Evelyn—I would've recognized her jet-black hair anywhere.

I kicked my feet against the ground, and when the paramedic put the stretcher inside the vehicle, Gavin had to restrain me from darting over to the ambulance. Evelyn was dead. We'd come to her house to end our friendship with her, and she was dead. My throat burned. Her life had been cut short. Dad's time had run out, and so had Evelyn's. And I couldn't help wondering about the future experiences Evelyn would never enjoy. Because Evelyn's mistakes seemed insignificant now. She was still human and hadn't deserved death.

CHAPTER 2

"Fucking bullshit," I said.

Gavin, Mona, Natalie, and I sat at a table in the back of the cafeteria while the chattering of numerous voices filled the air. It was the Monday after Evelyn had died.

Mona giggled. "Someone's feisty today."

My eyes remained glued on Mona while my glare intensified. "How am I supposed to react to my best friend's death being ruled an accident and not murder?"

Gavin belched after chugging more soda. "What makes you think Evelyn was murdered?"

"Falling down the stairs?" I asked sardonically. "She was a cheerleader, for fuck's sake."

"I'm not gonna cry over her death." Natalie scarfed down more salad. "Don't get me wrong—she didn't deserve to die. But I'm gonna give her the same consideration in death that she gave me in life."

Someone could've gutted me like a fish, and the pain wouldn't have compared to Natalie's comment. Not liking Evelyn was one thing, but Natalie could've been politer. Evelyn had still been a human being, despite her flawed past, and she certainly didn't deserve to be treated like she'd been nothing more than a rat scurrying through an alley.

"Sounds like a plan," Mona said.

"You guys don't feel guilty about wanting to end our friendship with her right before she died?" I asked.

Mona shrugged. "Nothing we do changes what happened. We saw her corpse in the body bag, so she's dead."

Ouch. Good to know Natalie wasn't the only one in the mood for being blunt. Refraining from the curtness wouldn't have killed Mona—it wasn't like I'd begged her to praise Evelyn. I just wanted something, anything that acknowledged the loss.

I snorted. "Nice."

Gavin smiled at me sympathetically. "But we're sorry you're hurting, and you can vent whenever you want."

How kind of him.

The lump in my throat refused to go away. "Thanks."

"Did you text or call your mother about Evelyn's death?" Mona asked.

I looked away. "No point in texting her when she's traveling for work."

"I'd love to be a pharmaceutical rep—I can just imagine all the things I'd do with the money," Natalie sighed.

"Other people in Greenwood have more money than me," I said.

"Still. Must be nice." Natalie finished the last bite of her salad, then threw the container in the trash.

"I'm sure your mother would want to hear from you if you're hurting because of Evelyn." Gavin nibbled on some chips, the crunching sounds growing louder with each bite.

"Whatever," I said.

Liam—who was sporting his usual blue and yellow Letterman jacket with the giant G emblazoned on one side—clipped by our table, carrying a lunch tray. His gaze met mine for a moment. My heart thumped louder and faster, and I averted my attention to my lunch tray before he moved on to sit with his football friends several tables behind ours.

Mona elbowed me. "What the fuck was that?"

"Didn't know you swore like a sailor," I said.

"Yeah, even I'm capable of an occasional surprise," she smirked.

I grunted. "No shit.".

Natalie drummed her fingers against the table. "Don't tell us anything you aren't comfortable revealing, but honesty might make you feel better."

"Excuse me?" I asked.

"When Natalie is right, she's right." Mona sipped her water. "Something happened between you two. You also can't pretend that look didn't happen."

"Don't know what you're talking about," I said.

Gavin raised an eyebrow. "Did he do something to you? I'll chat with him if you want."

Good to know Gavin had a brain, too—I never would've expected him to be so perceptive. He was closer to the truth than he could've realized, and there was a good chance that my friends might shake the truth out of me before lunch ended.

"I can defend myself," I said.

"He isn't bullying you, is he?" Natalie asked.

"Not exactly," I mumbled.

"What the hell does that mean?" Mona demanded.

I vigorously shook my head. "Doesn't matter. It's in the past."

Mona played with a strand of her hair, making the caramel highlights flash. "You'll feel a thousand pounds lighter after telling us what happened. Emotionally, that is."

I let out a long breath. "Fine," I said. "Maybe you're right."

"Telling us when it began might be a good starting point," Gavin prompted.

Someone's lunch tray clanked against the tile floor, and all four of their tacos spilled onto the ground. But I could hardly feel any sympathy for the person. My pulse hammered in my ears. I was going to be honest about my past with Liam—a past I'd wished away for the last four months—and I could only imagine how my friends would react.

"Well?" Gavin demanded.

I scratched the back of my neck while sweat dripped down my face. Deep breaths. Maybe revealing what happened with Liam would be cathartic. It wasn't like life could get any worse. "This whole thing started at the beginning of last May, at Evelyn's Spring Fling event. You know. The party you three didn't attend," I began.

I was in one of the empty guest bedrooms at Evelyn's Spring Fling party. I pressed END on my iPhone while music pulsed from a nearby room and the shuffling of footsteps echoed.

"Everyone is so fucking annoying," someone called out.

The person pushed the door open and entered the guest bedroom—Liam. He wore a short-sleeved Henley shirt, jeans, and white sneakers. And it was always impossible not to notice his spiked black hair. Liam might've been the one person who used more hair putty than me.

I shoved my iPhone into my pocket, then wiped my eyes.

"Sorry. Didn't realize this room was occupied," Liam said.

"Don't worry about it; I was leaving." I hurried towards the door.

Liam—who stood halfway between me and the door—tugged at my arm. But his touch didn't make my back hairs rise. Instead, the grip felt something like a parent holding their child's hand when crossing the street.

"Have you been crying?" he asked.

"Doesn't matter."

"It's a party. You're supposed to be having fun—AKA raiding my liquor cabinet."

I snickered. "Says the person looking for an empty room to escape the socializing."

"You're one to talk."

Damn. Liam was persistent. It wasn't enough for him to make just one comment about me being cooped up in a room and not having fun.

"I was taking a phone call." I brushed his arm off mine. "Not that it's any of your business."

"Wasn't trying to pry." Liam exhaled a breath. "But you'd feel the exact same way I did if you were me. I can only hear my friends bitch about how they're virgins for so long. If they're that sexually frustrated, they should try a dating app, am I right? Guess nobody welcomed them to the twenty-first century."

"Funny," I said.

A slow smile crept across Liam's face. "I know something that'd make you feel better."

"Doubtful."

"You haven't even heard my proposition." He placed his red Solo cup on the table behind him.

"You've got five seconds."

Liam stared into my eyes for a long time before pulling me in for a kiss. But he didn't just settle for a quick peck. Instead, he offered tongue and his fingers dragged across my cheeks, tracing the contours of my face.

I didn't know if he was kissing me because he'd had one too many drinks, but I didn't care. The kiss lasted a good five minutes before he kneeled. Liam looked into my eyes, then at my waist, then back into my eyes.

Beads of sweat dripped down my face. I'd watched enough movies and television shows to understand what was going to happen. But I didn't run out of the room, unable to breathe. I just nodded at him. Liam pulled my basketball shorts and boxers down to my ankles before moving his head towards my torso. His head and mouth bobbed faster and faster while my hands gripped the table behind me. I closed my eyes, moaning. This moment would end soon enough, but I'd make it last longer by tuning out the rest of the world.

Liam pulled his head back some time later and our eyes locked again. He bobbed his head, then I kneeled. Liam's plaid boxers and jeans dropped to his ankles in a matter of seconds and I leaned my head forward. He dug his fingers into my hair—harder than when he'd caressed my face. And Liam groaned at such a high pitch that we would've been caught if it weren't for the rap music blasting from the other room.

I strutted through the school hallway the Monday after Evelyn's Spring Fling party.

Liam stood next to two of his friends, who were about the same height as Liam, and towered over me by a good three or four inches. They had on the same Letterman jackets, jeans, T-shirts, and sneakers that Liam did.

I approached Liam. Nothing wrong with chatting with a new "friend"—it wasn't like I'd blab what had happened between us.

"Do you have a second, Liam?" I asked.

Liam yanked at his backpack strap. "I'm not going anywhere with you, faggot."

Jordon and Evan—Liam's friends—exchanged a look. Interesting. Good to know not all stereotypes were true, and some athletes were bothered by the use of a certain slur. It was more than I would've expected.

"Anything you wanna say to me, you can say in front of Jordon and Evan," Liam said.

I exhaled a breath. "I was just gonna tell you it was nice seeing you at Evelyn's party."

Liam blinked. "Come again, faggot?"

"I was wondering if you'd wanna hang sometime…?" I asked.

Liam snickered. "I don't chill with faggots—wouldn't want anyone thinking I was gay."

Evan bit his lip. "I don't think Connor is hitting on you."

"Seems harmless, man," Jordon said.

"Don't make excuses for the fucking pussy faggot," Liam said.

I fought back tears. My reaction was a little intense over someone I'd only kissed and had oral sex with, but I was only human. Liam might not have realized it, but he'd given me more than he knew that night. And a small part of me wished we could hook up again. That was, until Liam went on with his homophobic diatribe. I shouldn't have been attracted to someone who apparently wouldn't have given a fuck if a piano fell on me or if I got hit by a bus. A strong person would've had better self-control. But I couldn't help myself. I would always relish the fact that I'd gotten with someone who was hotter than me—everyone liked feeling desired in more than a platonic way. Was as natural as breathing.

"Calm down, Liam." Evan looked pained.

"Don't tell me what to do." Liam paused for a second. "It's time someone taught this faggot a lesson."

"Woah, why don't we just take a deep breath." Jordon held his hands up.

Liam tossed his backpack toward Evan. "Think you can manage holding my backpack, bitch? Or are you two faggots too busy thinking about jerking each other off?"

Ouch. Insulting me—a complete stranger—was one thing, but he should've respected Jordon and Evan. If he couldn't feign decency for them, then he wasn't the person I'd thought he was that night in the guest bedroom.

"I can look after it for a minute," Evan said.

Liam lunged toward me, threw me down on the floor, and started punching me. Over. And over. And over. It wasn't long before a metallic taste filled my mouth.

"That's enough," Evan said eventually, grabbing one of Liam's arms while Jordon grabbed the other.

Liam stumbled backward, thumping against the ground. But he was up again in a second, grabbing his backpack before I could even catch my breath.

Evan and Jordon helped me regain my feet. Liam dashed down the hallway and was soon out of sight.

Jordon frowned. "We're sorry about that. Liam just gets carried away."

"One way to put it," I said.

"He's not normally like this," Evan apologized. "His father has been giving him a harder time than usual and the steroids don't help, either."

"Understood," I said.

"I'm so sorry that happened to you," Gavin said, snapping me out of my reminiscence.

Mona picked at her nail. "Why didn't you tell us sooner?"

I bit my nail. "Duh. I was embarrassed."

Natalie patted my hand. "You didn't do anything wrong."

Gavin shot me a nervous glance. "Liam ever bother you again after that day?"

I scratched an itch on the back of my neck. "No. And I've been wondering if Jordon and Evan spoke to him later."

"You don't think Evelyn confronted Liam about the incident?" Mona asked.

"Don't think so." I cracked my knuckles. "She wasn't a witness, and I never told her what happened."

Natalie nodded. "What Liam did is seriously fucked up."

Mona cackled. "No shit. Although it's obvious why Liam acted the way he did."

"And why is that Dr. Freud?" Gavin asked.

I almost grinned at Gavin's comment. Gavin and Mona's banter was always a dependable source of serotonin. I might not have been dating anyone, but I could live vicariously through their relationship. My best friends deserved happiness, even if I couldn't have it. They were the embodiment of what a couple should be. Their dynamic toed the line between puppy love and cat-fighting. They could be interesting and exciting without hurting each other the way so many couples did on television shows and in books.

"He's a closet case suffering from internalized homophobia," Mona said.

"Also, I can confirm the steroid thing—I saw him inject in the locker room," Gavin added. "Not that I'm excusing his behavior."

"Right," I said.

Gavin scrunched his eyebrows. "I can't believe you two kissed and sucked each other off. Don't know what parties I've been attending, but they haven't been the right ones."

Mona waved at Gavin. "Have you forgotten your girlfriend is sitting next to you?"

Gavin smirked. "I'm teasing."

Liam got up from his table and walked towards ours.

"Fuck," I whispered.

Mona laid her hand over top of mine. "Don't worry. We won't let him say or do anything bad."

"Absolutely," Gavin agreed.

My pulse didn't soar out of control because Mona and Gavin were right. It was four against one, so Liam couldn't cause trouble. Even he couldn't have been that dumb.

"Hi, guys." Liam sat between Natalie and me. "I don't mean to interrupt, but the details of the funeral are still murky. You four will be the first to know, though, since you were some of Evelyn's best friends."

"Thanks," Mona said.

Liam rose without looking at me, returning to his table as quickly as he'd arrived.

"Awkward," Gavin whispered.

Mona nudged Gavin. "We'll support you with whatever your decision is, Connor. If you wanna attend the funeral and get closure, fine. But if you don't wanna deal with Liam, then that's fine too."

My breathing slowed. Good to know people were capable of changing—Mona's response was exactly what I needed. Whatever decision I made about attending the funeral, I had to be one-hundred percent certain.

I gritted my teeth. "I don't know…"

"At least you've got your haircut tomorrow evening," Natalie said.

I let out a breath. "Yeah, that's something. But I'm not only getting a trim. I wanna go platinum blond. Lord knows I've talked about it doing it for the longest time."

"If that'll make you happy," Mona said.

I left the hair salon the following evening.

A faint chill permeated the air, and the waxiness of the full moon glinted against the ground, providing extra lighting while I walked to my Mercedes.

Normally, I wouldn't have picked a 7:00 P.M. appointment, but it was all the hair salon had had on such short notice.

"The fuck you doing at a hair salon?" someone called.

I whipped my body around. Liam stood about ten feet from me.

"I've gotta go." I pulled out my car keys, then grabbed the car door handle.

"Please don't leave," he pleaded.

I looked over my shoulder, meeting his eyes. "Why would I do you any favors?"

"Because I wanted to apologize."

Wow. Lucky me, getting two surprises in less than a week. First Evelyn's death, now this. The only difference was that there was a chance this surprise would be wanted.

CHAPTER 3

Liam's eyes went round and soft. They reminded me of a guilty dog's. "I'm so sorry for punching you, man. You didn't deserve that, and the steroids weren't helping, either... thank goodness for Evan and Jordon, right?"

I stayed silent.

Liam tucked his hands into the pockets of his Letterman jacket. "I shouldn't have called you a faggot. That was a dick move."

My fingers tingled, but not because I wanted to get in my Mercedes and drive the hell away from Liam. His facial expression was still soft. It was like something palpable was radiating from his eyes, revealing everything worth knowing about his intentions. Someone like Liam—someone insecure about their sexuality—had no reason to fake an apology. Not being comfortable with himself meant talking to me—someone who was out—might've been a risk.

"Please say something," Liam begged.

Wind whipped through the parking lot, and a brief chill ran up my spine. Another reminder that it was basically fall, despite the calendar reading early September.

He lowered his gaze, breaking eye contact. "I wouldn't blame you if you hated me—I don't expect your forgiveness. Just thought you should know I was sorry."

Only one question lingered in my mind, and answering it was more necessary than carrying water when trekking through a desert. I didn't doubt that he was telling the truth, but I had no clue what his intentions were.

"Why now?" I asked.

Liam actually let out a sob. "It's the right thing to do. And… you were my sister's best friend."

My shoulders relaxed. "Thanks for apologizing. Couldn't have been easy for you."

He took a step forward, gripping his backpack strap. "Insulting you for going to a hair salon was also shitty. Blond looks great on you."

"Good to know."

"I'm serious. I hope you stick with blond."

"What are you even doing in town?" I asked, not knowing what else to say.

"I didn't have football practice today, so I decided to go to the library to work on homework." He made a brief fist. "Better than being home alone with my dad now Evelyn's dead. Although I should've planned for a ride."

"Anyway, sorry for your loss."

"Thanks."

I coughed, trying to clear the uneasiness. "Would you wanna come back to my house? My mother is out of state—she's not gonna be back for a few days."

My cheeks burned at my own proposition. Most people probably would've thought I was crazy for even talking to Liam after how he'd treated me. But I wasn't. Forgiveness was on my terms, not anyone else's. I also couldn't forget about how Mona, Natalie, and Gavin had acted at lunch the other day. Supporting me with whatever decision I made about attending the funeral wasn't enough. Shedding at least one tear over Evelyn's death wasn't complicated. So, yeah. Liam's company offered me something Mona, Natalie, and Gavin's didn't. A high that surpassed any drug, because I had no qualms about a little impulsiveness with Liam. I wasn't injecting myself with dangerous substances—I just couldn't be alone for another evening. Besides, Liam was the one person who might've understood how dealing with Evelyn's death felt. I wouldn't have wanted to be judged for one moment of stupidity either if the roles were reversed. It wasn't like his punch had required medical attention.

"You're comfortable enough to be alone with me in your own home?" Liam asked. "Aren't afraid I'm gonna beat you to a fucking pulp?"

I wrinkled my nose.

"It was a joke," Liam said.

"I know."

Liam moaned against my neck before collapsing on me, our hands locking together and then pulling apart as he slid off. He flopped back on the right side of the bed.

"Damn!" Liam exclaimed.

I wiped sweat from my forehead. "That's one word for it. Two, actually."

"I can't believe I waited this long before going all the way with someone."

"Interesting."

He leaned toward me and rested his free hand under his chin. "Was that your first time going all the way too?"

I nodded.

Liam sucked in a breath and blew it out, slow. "I wasn't lying about my apology."

I finally made eye contact with him. "I can take you home, if you want."

"Trying to get rid of me?" he asked.

Hopefully, Liam wasn't a poker player. He would've suffered an awful lot of losses if he was. The puppy-dog look was back in his eyes. And I was once again reminded of how Liam was still human—like

Evelyn—despite his flaws. I almost sighed in relief—it seemed like Liam had enjoyed what just happened between us.

"Nope. I just don't expect you to stay the night," I said.

"We still have ten hours before we gotta go to school."

I chuckled. "We aren't gonna fuck like rabbits all night long. Need some sleep."

He smirked. "One more time wouldn't hurt."

"Careful. I might think you care."

"What we did tonight doesn't mean I'm gay—I'm not," Liam blurted.

There it was. The jab that was worse than a spear's would've been, because I should've known it was coming. Perhaps I'd gotten my hopes up by assuming Liam and I had formed a genuine connection tonight. It was fine. Liam would need time to accept his sexuality. That type of thing wouldn't happen overnight.

"But I promise not to lash out at you in public," he said.

"How considerate. The only thing missing from this conversation is a 'no homo.'"

"I'm not the same guy I was back in May—violence isn't the answer."

"I don't think anyone would care if you were gay," I said.

"My dad would."

My heart almost skipped a beat. Another mitigating factor. Wanting a parent's unconditional love was as natural as the sun's rising and setting. Mom might've been a little absent from my life because of her job, but she accepted my bisexuality—I didn't know what I would've done if she hadn't. Being a teen with homework, classes, SATs, and college applications was tough enough already.

"For the record, you can label yourself whatever you want," I said.

Liam squeezed my hand. "Thanks."

Touching my hand wasn't much, but the most intimate gestures were sometimes the least sexual. So, I didn't push Liam's hand away. It was better than nothing. I just needed something, anything, to make me feel less alone.

CHAPTER 4

I was exiting the kitchen the evening after sleeping with Liam when the doorbell rang. I opened the door. Liam stood on my front porch, sporting his usual attire—Letterman jacket, jeans, T-shirt, sneakers.

My jaw dropped a little. It probably looked dumb. "What are you doing here?"

Wind rattled in through the doorway, creating a brief chill.

"I just came from football practice," Liam said.

"Okay…"

"You said your mother would be out of town for a few."

"And?" I asked.

He bit his lower lip. "Can I please come in?"

I threw a glance inside, then Liam stepped into my home. The front door clicked as I locked it. I turned around to face him.

Liam looked me over and let out a breath. "Have you been crying?"

I swiped at one of my eyes, face warming. "Yeah, but it's not important."

"I've been thinking about last night," he stammered after a minute.

I suppressed laughter. An amused reaction would've been cruel, even when dealing with Liam. He hadn't done anything to make me doubt his apology—like getting too rough in bed or punching me again. And that was worth something. Not because I was settling for less than I deserved, but because Liam might get the opportunity Evelyn never did. To prove he was worth something.

My eyebrows inched up. "You wanna hook up again, don't you?"

Liam didn't break our eye contact. "I'm not gay…"

"Like I said last night, I'm not gonna tell you who you are."

"Thanks," he murmured.

"Why don't we go to my bedroom?" I asked.

He nodded at me without speaking. But I didn't pout at the silence. A small part of me was reveling in the reversal of power dynamics. He was the popular, athletic guy while I was the shy photographer. Yet he wanted something that only I had the power to give him.

"Make yourself comfortable," I said after closing my bedroom door.

Liam continued standing while I looked into his black eyes. A scorching sensation jabbed my stomach, stronger than heartburn. Mona was a lot of things, but she could definitely read people. Liam's eye-fucking was so intense that my body was beyond shaking. I'd never known such intense staring was possible.

"I'll make this easier for you." I lifted my T-shirt from my body, then threw it onto the floor. "You want me."

"You've got no idea." Liam kissed me without wincing, hands once again on my cheeks while I inhaled the earthy sweetness of whatever deodorant he used.

My hands traveled to Liam's waist, then they were ripping his T-shirt off and tossing it where mine lay crumpled on the floor.

There should've been cringing—I had no doubt some people would've judged me for hooking up with Liam again. But the rush of blood pumping through my veins was my only thought. Liam offered fun, and I would accept it.

"Fucking amazing," Liam panted sometime later while sitting on the right side of the bed.

I grabbed a tissue from the mahogany nightstand to the left of me to rub sweat off my forehead and smiled at Liam.

"Glad you enjoyed yourself," I said.

His jaw twitched. "I hope you know you can be honest with me—I'd never judge you. Besides, I wouldn't betray your confidence."

"Gonna have to be more specific."

"I'm referring to the crying when you answered the door."

"Oh…"

He caressed my right cheek. "I might be closeted, but you're the one who can't make eye contact with me half the time. Do you hate me that much?"

"You can't honestly care about my problems."

"Listening to other people bitch is a good distraction. In small doses, that is."

"True."

Liam snorted. "Being tipsy the night of Evelyn's Spring Fling party didn't erase my memory. You cried then, too."

"Your point?"

"Something's bothering you," he said.

"Fine. I'll tell you."

Liam sat up straighter, shifting around on the mattress. "I'm listening."

Shock still had my body in its grasp. If I didn't know better, I would've guessed I was in a parallel universe. It was unthinkable that Liam was interested in me whining about my problems. I wasn't even interested enough in them myself to complain about them. It was probably best that I drop the skepticism, though. Venting could help— even if the vent was to Liam Sinclair. I couldn't deny that I hadn't yet unpacked Dad's death. That I was pretending the pain didn't exist. A better person would've insisted on leaving the party and visiting Dad at the hospital right away. But no. Instead, I'd kissed and done worse with Liam. And I'd have to live with choosing pleasure over my family for the rest of my life.

"Today would've been my father's forty-third birthday, and my mother didn't even text about it," I said. "But this goes back to Evelyn's Spring Fling. The phone call I took that night was from my mother. My father had a heart attack and was in the hospital."

"Sorry, man."

"I haven't gotten to the worst part," I said.

"I'm listening."

I sucked on my teeth. "My mother didn't have a problem with me staying at the party—she said to stop at the hospital in the morning even though she'd decided to keep my dad company overnight. Except when I arrived the next morning, my dad wasn't there. They'd already taken him to the morgue."

Tears trickled down my cheeks. No point in filtering my emotions now I was getting all this out. Liam had nothing to gain by using my information or feelings against me. It felt very intimate, just the two of us alone in my bedroom. Almost as if the room was our own little world.

"That fucking blows," Liam said.

"No need to state the obvious, but yeah. Not getting to stay goodbye sucks."

"Thank you for telling me." Liam stretched his arms. "My father might be alive, but I still lost a mother. She died of a heart attack, too."

My lips curled. "Damn."

"She was a two-pack-a-day smoker for a good twenty years. Fucking cigarettes."

I somehow liked seeing Liam's anger about his mother's death. It made him just a little more human. Made me feel less shitty about sleeping with him.

I tossed Liam his boxers and jeans. "This was fun, but I should go to bed soon."

"I'm crushed you don't want me to stay the night."

"You'll live."

"I didn't sneak out before you woke up in the morning. I could've, but I didn't."

"Do you want a medal?" I asked.

"It's nice having someplace different to sleep."

"That scared of your father?" I asked.

Liam grunted. "Don't ask questions you don't want the answers to."

"You can stay." I drew in a deep breath. "But don't expect me to cook you breakfast in the morning."

"Wouldn't dream of it."

"This also… can't happen again. This was the last time."

"Whatever you say."

"I'm serious, William."

Liam hissed at me. "Don't call me William—it's pretentious. Liam is more badass."

"I was teasing."

He patted my nose. "I know."

Thank goodness Liam's internalized homophobia and whatever aggression he might've built up after Evelyn's death hadn't given him a stick up his ass. Nobody should take themselves too seriously—myself included.

"Is there a date for the service yet?" My head collapsed onto the pillow behind me, and my arms dropped to my sides.

Liam reached over tentatively, then stroked my hair. I didn't swat his hand away. Instead, I closed my eyes, waiting for a response.

"Saturday," Liam finally said. "And I'd love it if you came."

I would've exploded into laughter if I didn't want to protect Liam's feelings. He almost sounded like a needy boyfriend. That provided me a brief comfort. It was like coming home from work and discovering the chicken had already been taken out of the freezer to defrost. Everyone wanted to be needed, although I wondered who might end up getting more attached. Liam. Or me.

"Won't your father be pissed by me being there?" I asked. "You know, since I'm out."

"He'll be too wrapped up in his own feelings. He won't even care if you're there as long as you don't do something gay."

"Good to know."

"Be nice to have a familiar face," Liam said.

"Your buddies from football and lacrosse aren't coming?"

"They aren't my friends."

I laughed. "Could've fooled me. You didn't answer my question, though."

"They don't even know the real me."

"Excuse me?"

"You're the only one who's ever seen the real me." He continued running his fingers through my hair. I wasn't sure if he was doing it because he thought I was still upset about my father or because he needed a distraction. Something to silence the rage at having to say goodbye to Evelyn. "Promise me you'll think about coming."

Perhaps appeasing Liam was my best option. There was no need to ruin the moment. Liam would never become my boyfriend, but I could enjoy our fleeting interactions for what they were. An escape from the loneliness. Anything to make the constant feeling of impending dread less palpable.

"Sure," I said.

In spite of my doubts, I attended the funeral.

It wasn't even about doing something nice for Liam—I didn't owe him anything. Being at Evelyn's funeral provided an opportunity for closure. Something I didn't get when Dad died—it'd been hard to worry about my own feelings when supporting Mom was my top priority.

I sat in the back row of the church—it was important to be close to the exit in case I got overwhelmed—while the pastor stood by his podium at the front of the church, humming about how fleeting life was.

Being alone might've been the most significant thing about the whole affair. Mom's boss had extended her latest business trip, and I hadn't asked Mona, Gavin, or Natalie to accompany me to the service. No point in forcing them to do something they didn't want to. Not if they'd only be making passive-aggressive comments about Evelyn the whole time. It would've been a waste of their time and energy.

My gaze shifted to the right of the pastor. More specifically, to the wooden casket. It was closed, but there was a blown-up photo of Evelyn beside it. The image was of Evelyn in a white dress, her wavy, black hair extending several inches past her chest.

The pastor continued babbling his eulogy, but the most important conversation I'd ever had with Evelyn burned in my mind, keeping his words at bay.

I was in the eighth grade, standing by my locker one morning before homeroom, when Evelyn strutted towards me.

She grinned. "I've been meaning to talk to you about something."

"Something bad?"

Evelyn giggled. "Don't be ridiculous. And please stop thinking it's a bad thing whenever someone wants to talk to you."

"Okay. What's up?"

"I've seen the way you look at male actors in tabloids. You know. When you think nobody is watching."

I stayed silent.

"I'm not trying to embarrass you," Evelyn continued. "Just wanted to let you know you've got nothing to be ashamed of. You're great just the way you are."

Tears dotted my eyes as the pastor continued his eulogy.

I was more tempted to leave the service than I should've been. The urge to excuse myself was only natural, though. Evelyn had given me the confidence to be who I was. Living the next sixty or seventy years without her, the way I had to with Dad… I didn't know what I was going to do.

So, fuck it. Evelyn was the first person who would've told me it was okay to leave the service and pull myself together. And that was exactly what I did. I rose, my stomach tightening into a knot, and dashed to the exit.

My shoes squeaked against the floor as I arrived at the bathroom.

Water trickled from the sink for a few moments. I splashed it on my face, not even looking at my reflection.

The door opened, then the lock clicked.

I turned the water off before cocking my head. Liam stood next to me. He offered a smile.

"Just wanted to check on you. Saw you ducking out in the middle of the eulogy."

"Shouldn't I be checking on you?" I asked.

"Doesn't matter. Point is, we're alone again."

Liam shuffled forward, then kissed me. His fingers moved across my cheeks and he pushed his tongue deep and hard into my mouth.

I pulled back after a second, pushing down the desire growing in me.

"What's wrong?" he asked.

"I'm not gonna blow you or have sex in a church bathroom. Definitely not during Evelyn's service."

Liam surveyed the space. "It's pretty clean compared to most public bathrooms."

"Not the point."

He leaned into my right ear, massaging my shoulders. "When can I see you again?"

"My mom is still out of town."

"Perfect," Liam whispered, voice prickling my skin. "I'll stop by at some point in the evening."

"You should go before someone becomes suspicious."

Liam snickered. "Careful. Might think you care."

I gave Liam a mock frown before he kissed me goodbye. The lock clicked, and he was gone as fast as he'd arrived.

I might not have known what Liam and I were doing, but one fact remained certain. I owed it to Evelyn to investigate her death. Falling down the stairs and dying out of sheer clumsiness seemed too random and convenient. Evelyn had been there for me in life, and I'd be there for Evelyn in her death. If there were more sinister details lurking beneath the surface of her passing, then I was going to unearth them.

CHAPTER 5

Sunlight radiated from the cloudless sky the following Monday afternoon as I walked onto the football field. I'd stayed an hour past the end of the school day because 3:15 P.M. was when cheerleading practice ended. The cheerleaders were a few yards away from the football players, who were lounging instead of practicing.

Liam exchanged a stolen glance with me, and my heart raced. But my cheeks weren't flushed because of Liam. He wasn't the reason I was visiting the football field. The girl I stood in front of—Violet Judd—was why. Violet had been one of Evelyn's best friends from the cheerleading squad. She might've known something about Evelyn—something that could help prove that Evelyn falling down the stairs had been murder, not an accident.

Violet giggled after finishing her water. "Can I help you with something?"

"I'm sorry," I stuttered. "I don't mean to be rude. Just wanted to chat for a minute."

Violet peeked at the gold watch looped around her right wrist, then looked up. "Sure. I've got time before my dad arrives."

"Sucks that Evelyn is dead."

"Tell me about it."

"This question might be kinda weird…"

Violet's blonde pigtails bobbed in the wind. "Can't be worse than a parade of football players always looking to hook up with me."

I wished I was a snake and could shed my skin. I didn't need to be a girl to sympathize with her. A person only needed to turn on the TV or read a newspaper to understand what girls and women grappled with on a regular basis.

"I was wondering if you knew something about Evelyn," I said.

"Excuse me?"

"Don't you think it's odd that she randomly fell down the stairs and died?"

"What are you saying?"

I leaned closer. "Appearances aren't everything. Maybe she told you something she didn't tell anyone else."

Violet stared off at the sky for a few seconds as if making up her mind about something. "Actually… I might be able to help."

I blinked. "Really?"

"But you can't tell anyone what I'm gonna tell you."

Now my face was really glowing. Violet was close to telling me something juicy. My theory that someone had murdered Evelyn by pushing her down the stairs had to be correct.

I made a gesture over my chest. "Cross my heart."

"She was dating an older guy. In fact, they'd meet at Chuck's for drinks almost every Thursday since they don't card."

"How old are we talking?"

Violet shrugged. "I don't know. She never told me who the guy was."

"Could he have been in college?" I asked.

"Don't think so. She never outright said it, but I kind of wondered if the guy was *way* older than her."

"Like a married man?" I asked.

Making the jump to Evelyn being involved with a married man wasn't a stretch. Not to me, at least. If Evelyn was being secretive about a relationship, then that'd be a reason why. Stranger things happened all the time.

"Possibly." She glanced at her watch before sucking in a long breath. "Wish I could chat more, but I gotta go. Nice talking, though, so let me know if you ever wanna grab a coffee."

Violet was gone in a matter of seconds, growing smaller and smaller in the distance until she'd disappeared through the football field's metal gate into the parking lot.

Liam jogged over to me, a smirk twisting his mouth. "What are you doing here, man?"

"Had a question for Violet." I put my hands on my hips. "Anyway, you're taking a big risk being seen with me in public—wouldn't want anyone getting the wrong idea about you."

"I wanted to apologize."

I shouldn't have felt shocked again after his apology to me outside the salon, but I couldn't help myself. It really seemed like Liam cared about being a better person. The old Liam—the one who'd had no problem with homophobic outbursts—probably wouldn't have apologized if someone had offered him all the money in the world. No fabricating that kind of rage.

"For what?" I asked.

"For not stopping by your house after the funeral. I wasn't trying to be a dick."

My eyebrows knitted together. "You're not my boyfriend, Liam. You don't have to like, account for your whereabouts to me."

"Didn't want you to think I was avoiding you. My dad can just be a handful sometimes."

I leaned forward and let my lips graze his ear. "Afraid I'm gonna start sleeping with someone else?"

Liam didn't frown, kick his feet, shove me, or have any kind of outburst. And it almost made my jaw drop to the ground. Someone with Liam's demeanor should've worried about how a guy invading their personal space would look to others. Instead, Liam cackled.

"Why? Got a better offer?" he asked.

My mouth remained near his right ear. "If you want something from me, then you're gonna have to ask nicely."

"Mom still out of town? Was hoping we could hang again."

"She got back yesterday afternoon, but she'll leave for her next trip tomorrow morning."

"Perfect. I'll come by your house tomorrow night."

"Admit it—you want me?" I demanded.

"Yeah," Liam said under his breath, the response so soft it was almost inaudible.

I nearly bit my tongue—in a literal sense, not a figurative one. Gavin's gaze was glued to me from where he stood at the opposite end of the football field.

I'd be fine, though. It wasn't like Gavin could tell Liam and I were sleeping together just from how close we were to each other. Close enough that my heart couldn't stop fluttering. Because I wanted nothing more than to kiss Liam. But I couldn't. Not in public.

My arrangement with Liam was something I'd ultimately orchestrated for myself. Something that helped me escape the pain both of losing my father early in life and of Evelyn dying. And if nobody else knew about my dynamic with Liam, then variables couldn't ruin it. Like Gavin babbling his concern to Natalie and Mona, and them deciding to stage an "intervention." As if they were perfect. I still hadn't forgotten about how they'd shown more feeling for the school district canceling February Break last year than for Evelyn's death.

Liam leaned forward under the bed comforter nestled around us the following evening. His eyes were wide.

"Something wrong?" I asked.

"You were joking, right?"

"About what?"

"Yesterday," he croaked.

"You're gonna have to provide more context."

"You wouldn't start sleeping with someone else, would you?" He gripped the bed comforter harder.

Liam had done some provoking things in the past, but now he was really making me want to pull my hair out. If anything, I should've been the one getting attached. Not him. People were capable of surprising you, though. Like the woman who fought with her daughter-in-law, only to weep when she was dying of cancer. The only question was how much Liam would allow himself to feel for me, because I wouldn't lie. I was curious about how far this dynamic would go. I didn't have shit for brains, so I understood that we couldn't keep sleeping together forever, no matter how loud Liam moaned against my neck. This arrangement would end the same way everything else in life did. It wasn't like Liam would ever come out of the closet.

"Someone's anxious," I said.

Liam huffed. "Forget it."

"What? Don't believe I was just chatting with Violet?"

"Liar isn't the word I used, but…"

I shook my head. "Never thought you were the jealous type."

"I'm not." Liam placed his head down on the pillow, then tucked his left arm by the side of his head, stare lingering.

Liam could deny the accusation as many times as he wanted, but he couldn't fool me. His cheeks had turned bright red. Maybe, just maybe, my earlier theory about him was true. His failure to embrace his sexuality didn't mean I meant nothing to him. We would just never become a couple, and that was fine. Fun was the only thing I needed from him.

"Not everything is a sexual transaction, Liam."

He snorted. "Whatever."

"Besides, you're handful enough."

"Damn straight." Liam kissed me on the lips.

I stared at the ceiling after Liam kissed me. It was the only thing I could do. I wasn't sure how to feel about him kissing me. In a way, kissing created more intimacy than actually sleeping together—the gesture showed affection, even if only in a small way. But nothing good would come from accepting more than sex from Liam. Liam would never be able to love me unless he loved himself.

I was twisting in my locker combination the next morning before first period when Mona, Natalie, and Gavin approached.

Gavin gave me a weak smile. "Hi, buddy."

"Something wrong?" I asked.

Mona rolled her eyes. "We agreed I'd do the talking."

"Sorry," Gavin said.

Natalie's hair fell behind her shoulders as she flicked her neck. "Be nice, Mona."

"Always am."

Natalie snorted. "Whatever you say."

My lungs might as well have been filled with water. I didn't need to be psychic to know what they wanted to confront me about. I could've kicked myself. I shouldn't have ignored the possibility that Gavin might get wise after my exchange with Liam on the football field yesterday.

But maybe I was wrong. I was only seventeen years old, after all, and didn't know everything. Mona might've wanted to ask me for Mom's famous lasagna recipe, not give me the ass-whooping of the century.

"We know you're sleeping with Liam," Mona said.

Okay. Not lasagna. I folded my arms. "You've got no idea what you're talking about."

"You aren't gonna deny it?" Natalie asked.

"Natalie, please!" Mona hissed.

I turned to Gavin. "Did you have to blab to them about yesterday?"

"He did the right thing," Natalie said.

"For once, Natalie's right," Mona agreed. "We don't wanna see you do something stupid. You can do much better than a closet case."

I looked down at the floor. "I can't believe you figured out what's going on from one little interaction."

"No straight guy lets another guy invade his personal space like that unless it's a hug," Gavin said.

"You've gotta breakup with him," Mona added.

Forcing deep breath after deep breath into my body was the only thing I could do. No amount of anger made having a meltdown okay. Getting called to the principal or my guidance counselor for going "Girl Interrupted" on my friends' asses wasn't exactly college essay material.

"He apologized," I said.

"Stockholm Syndrome isn't a good look, hon," Mona said.

Needing to vent my frustration somehow, I screamed. "You've got no fucking clue what you're talking about!"

Mona looked taken aback. "Excuse me?"

"I'm not joking. Liam's apology is more than you three ever did for me," I said.

"What are you getting at?" Gavin demanded.

"My father's death sound familiar?" I pointed to Gavin and Mona. "You two were gonna take me out to dinner a couple of days after he died, but you went to a Green Day concert instead." I threw a look at Natalie next. "And *you* were supposed to come with me to my dad's funeral but were too hungover from a night partying to drag your ass out of bed."

Mona adjusted her frayed headband. "We might've fucked up…"

I scoffed. Please. If my friendship had meant anything to Mona, she wouldn't have vacillated on the issue. Real friends didn't need to be told to apologize. Called being a decent person, for fuck's sake.

"You think?" I raised my voice.

"You should've said something sooner," Gavin said.

I chuckled. "Wow."

Natalie pressed her hands together. "You deserved better, and that's gonna change starting right now. Evelyn's death clearly brings up triggers for you, stuff about your father."

"We offered to attend Evelyn's funeral with you," Gavin said.

"Probably to judge her," I yelled louder. "You wanna know what I think?"

"I've got a feeling you're gonna tell us anyway," Mona sighed.

What a cow. She and the others fucked up, and I wouldn't ignore their behavior just because they were my "best friends."

"You act like Evelyn is this terrible person, but you three are nothing but a bunch of self-righteous hypocrites," I said.

Relief flooded me. Somehow, I'd actually said what I thought. Accepting that people were flawed was fair, but there was nothing worse than hypocrisy. If Natalie, Mona, and Gavin were gonna act a certain way, then they needed to own their behavior. Life was too short to do otherwise.

Gavin touched the scruff on his cheeks. "Can see why you think that."

"What do you want from us?" Mona asked.

"Nothing," I blurted. "I don't wanna hear from you or see you ever again."

Natalie raised her eyebrows. "You don't mean that," she said.

The warning bell rang, but I wasn't going to bitch about first period starting. Even Algebra 2 was better than talking to these three morons. But I'd leave them with one final word. I had to reinforce the anger coiling inside of me, because I was nobody's victim anymore—not even in a small way.

"I do. Anyway, I'm fucking done with you three." I stuffed my books into my backpack and slammed my locker shut. Without another word, I rushed away from Mona, Natalie, and Gavin.

Sometimes, loneliness was the best option. At least then I only had myself to blame if I was disappointed.

CHAPTER 6

Moonlight trickled through the kitchen window beside the stove.

Around twelve hours had passed since my conversation with Natalie, Mona, and Gavin, but my pulse drummed in my ears as if it had been five minutes ago. I couldn't believe how self-righteous they were. It wasn't like they had a reason to be concerned about me. Liam and I were only hooking up, not in a committed relationship. Although I almost chuckled thinking about how I was still sleeping with Liam even after vowing to end whatever was happening between us. He was a weakness, and I couldn't help myself. I couldn't forget about Liam's apology, either—proof of his self-awareness.

The doorbell rang, so I went to answer it. Liam stood on my front porch, hands in his Letterman jacket pockets.

"Were we supposed to meet up tonight?" I asked. "Because I didn't get a text from you."

He hung his head. "I didn't know where else to go. Your mom still away on another business trip?"

"I see. And, yeah, my mother won't be back for a few days."

"May I please come in?" Liam was almost sobbing.

One glance at his puffy lip—which was coated in blood—assured me that Liam wasn't playing a game. I gesticulated at him and he entered my home. Back in the kitchen, I pulled an icepack from the freezer, then tossed it. Liam caught it and placed it on his lip.

"Do I even wanna know what happened?" I asked.

"It's a long story."

I drew in a deep breath. "I already finished my homework, so I got plenty of time."

"What a surprise."

"Please tell me you didn't start a fight."

"You think that little of me?"

I didn't respond. Instead, I whistled. It was great that he wanted to be a better person, but I hadn't gotten a lobotomy. I couldn't completely forget about my past with Liam, no matter how grateful I might've been for his apology.

"Sorry," Liam continued. "Should've known better than to ask that."

"If something happened, you can tell me. I promise it stays in this room."

"I came home from football practice. My dad was in the living room." Liam paused for a second, shivering as wind slammed against the house. "It wasn't even seven o'clock, and he'd already finished half a 750-milliliter bottle of whiskey."

"I don't understand."

"He got all up in my face. Spouting shit about how he wished Evelyn was alive and I was the one who died."

I clapped my hands to my face. "I'm so sorry."

"Then he started punching me."

I cringed. Empathy wasn't as difficult as Algebra 2 in this situation—no child deserved to be beaten by their parent. It defied the natural order of life. Liam's father should've been the one person who always believed in him. I didn't have a magic wand to wave away the pain, so I'd have to accept that Liam might be as broken as me. Mom and Dad might never have hit me, but I was still packed with rage from Dad's death—rage that Liam must've felt when his father beat him.

So Liam and I were more alike than I'd imagined. We'd both had our innocence stolen from us. Surviving wasn't living, no matter how much someone tried spinning the situation.

"Does he get like this a lot?" I asked.

"Yes," Liam mumbled. A couple of tears even rolled down from his eyes. Wow. Never thought I'd witness Liam Sinclair crying.

"Thank you for telling me."

"Here." Liam threw the icepack back at me, and I almost didn't catch it.

"I'm not trying to be an asshole, but why come to me?"

"Isn't it obvious? You're the only one I can trust."

I got what he was saying, even though he didn't elaborate more. If Liam was able to trust me with his closeted status, then he must've realized he could tell me anything.

"Have you eaten dinner yet?" I asked.

"Appreciate it, but I'm not hungry." He coughed. "There was one thing I was hoping for, though."

I would've smiled at Liam if the revelation he'd made moments earlier hadn't been so serious. I couldn't ignore the paradox of Liam being unable to get enough of me even while closeted. Refusal to act on same-sex-oriented desires would've been a logical course of action for someone in denial about their sexuality. But life was more complicated than that, and Liam could be disgusted by who he was even while giving in to it.

"Really?" I asked.

"Only if you're in the mood. I know you aren't my rent-a-hooker."

I let out a faint laugh. "Thanks, I think."

"I don't wanna be alone."

"Sure. We can sleep together again."

Liam scurried towards me without another word before kissing me. I didn't tell him to slow down as his kisses became more intense. I just let myself become intoxicated by the usual earthy, sweet scent of whatever deodorant he used — really was gonna have to find out the name of it.

He scooted closer to me while we were lying under the comforter afterward.

"I'm serious about you not telling anyone about my father," Liam said.

"I know, I know."

Liam's revelation that his dad was physically abusive and possibly a drunk wasn't the only secret lingering on my mind. I couldn't stop thinking about Liam being in the closet now that Mona, Natalie, and Gavin knew about our affair. It was possible I needed to chat with them about keeping Liam's secret. They didn't even have to care about me. They just needed to care about the implications of outing a closeted person. More specifically, I had to make sure they wouldn't blab about Liam's sexuality all over school, no matter how much they snarled at the thought of Liam and I hooking up.

Liam crossed his arms over his chest. "Sometimes I think about what my life would've been like if my father wasn't such an asshole. Not everyone wakes up in the morning wanting to be evil, you know? Some monsters are just made."

Monsters. It was an interesting word. The label was an even deeper self-reflection than Liam's apology to me that night in front of the salon. It made my heart ache for him. If Liam didn't believe in himself, then nobody would.

"Even bad things end," I said.

"Fantastic." Liam's head collapsed onto my chest—something he'd never done before—but I didn't shove him off. Instead, my fingers snaked through his spiked black hair while his breathing slowed.

Liam and I didn't have much, but we had my bedroom. And that was something. It was still our own little world where things like Liam being in the closet, his horrible father, and Evelyn's death didn't matter. Everyone needed to pretend once in a while.

I approached my friends where they stood in front of Gavin's locker the following morning.

Gavin crossed his arms. "Come to apologize for yesterday?"

Natalie jabbed Gavin's arm. "Don't be presumptuous."

Thank goodness for Natalie. She seemed to at least feel bad, which meant she wasn't as terrible as Mona and Gavin. They probably wouldn't even acknowledge they'd done something wrong.

"There's something you can do for me," I said.

Mona played with her ponytail. "If you're gonna tell us to go to hell, then you can save your energy."

I gave Mona a scornful look. "Wasn't what I was gonna say. Probably don't have to remind you that nobody can know about Liam."

"You want us to keep your dirty secret?" Gavin said.

Gavin might've been a bigger jackass than I'd realized. Labeling my interactions with Liam "dirty" was too much. Our dynamic might've been a secret, but no shame pulsed through my body. Life was too short to be moving backwards. Liam gave me pleasure, and I'd always be thankful for that.

Natalie wrapped her pearl necklace around her fingers. "You don't even have to ask, Connor."

"Look, man," Gavin said. "We'd like to put yesterday behind us. Whaddya say?"

"Your hypocrisy isn't the only thing," I said. "I didn't even mention all the things I've done for you. Like tutoring you in Geometry last year, taking Mona shopping, and always being around when Natalie wanted boy-talk. But you know why I did those things? Because you're my friends. And if your loved ones made a mistake like Liam did when he punched me, then I bet you'd be advocating for a second chance."

Mona pursed her lips. "What more do you want from us?"

"Nothing. Just keep Liam's secret." I darted down the hallway and away from Mona, Natalie, and Gavin.

I had no regret about not accepting their sort-of-apology. They couldn't admit I had a right to be involved with whoever I wanted. I mean, sure, we'd probably become friends again at some point. But I wouldn't speed up the reconciliation. Not until they were more genuine about their remorse.

I sat on bed with my feet up after school, contemplating what Violet had revealed to me the other day as afternoon sunlight filtered in through my jungle-pattern curtains. Learning that Evelyn might've been involved with an older guy was a good first step, but I needed to figure out what I'd do next.

A tilt of my head turned out to be all I needed for that. The Sue Grafton book *"A" is for Alibi* sitting on a stack of papers on my desk caught my eye. The book had been Evelyn's. She'd lent the novel to me, even though it was signed by Sue Grafton. So I had a reason to stop by Liam's house—Liam and his father might want the book back to sell or keep as a memory of Evelyn even if they didn't plan on reading it. And Evelyn had once told me they kept an extra key under the doormat out front.

I stood in Evelyn's bedroom half an hour later, the book already placed on Evelyn's wooden desk. It was covered in papers, other books, miscellaneous trinkets, and thick layers of cobwebs.

My throat tightened. This was my first time in Evelyn's room since she'd died. So, yeah. I needed a moment to fight back tears. I'd always be shocked that Evelyn had died so young. It didn't matter how trite the idea sounded—her life had truly been cut too short.

Anyway, Liam and his father weren't home, so I'd gone with the key-under-the-doormat plan.

Even though I'd technically broken into Liam's house, I felt no shakiness, no sweat dripping down my back. It was possible that even if Liam's father caught me, he'd be too consumed by his own feelings to care. My sudden surge of courage was also proof that something positive was coming from me spending time with Liam. If I had the confidence to pursue a guy who was out of my league, I might've been capable of doing anything.

I grinned after spotting Evelyn's diary on top of her bookcase—I recognized the gold-coated pages that Evelyn had described to me once.

I flipped through the diary. It didn't take a lot of scanning for me to learn that Violet had been right. Evelyn didn't reveal the identity of the man, but she copped to him being married and in his forties, in addition to the fact that he still went to Chuck's on the Thursdays when Evelyn couldn't meet up.

"The fuck you doing here?" Someone called out.

I lifted my gaze from the diary, then bit my lip. Liam was standing in the doorway.

CHAPTER 7

I flung the diary onto Evelyn's bed, then walked toward Liam and looped my arms around his neck.

Liam didn't remove my arms. Instead, his Adam's apple throbbed while our gazes held. "Well?"

"I came because I just had to have you," I said.

Liam gave me a look. "You're in Evelyn's room, not mine."

"So? What's the big deal if I want to come in here for a minute? It's the only thing that's left of her."

"Okay."

"And Evelyn told me about the spare key under the doormat." I kissed Liam without giving the issue another thought. He looped his arms around me, and the kissing became more vigorous with each passing second.

He pulled back after a beat.

"What?" I asked.

"You aren't telling me the truth."

"Excuse me?"

"You're trying to use sex to distract me, and it won't work."

I might've punched a wall if the action wouldn't have resulted in a visit to the ER. If the universe was on my side, Liam would've gone along with having sex. Sleeping with him was easier than sharing my theory about Evelyn's death. No telling how he would react to me proposing the possibility of murder.

"What would you know about that?" I asked.

"My mother did that with my father when she was alive."

"That's a conversation I don't wanna have."

He wove his arms together. "I might be a jock, but I'm not a moron. You were holding Evelyn's diary."

I let out a nervous laugh. "You caught me. I love snooping."

"That's not it."

"You're reading more into the situation than you should. Let it go."

"Telling when someone is lying is easy."

"If you think I'm a liar, then I'm leaving. I'm not some random conquest." I scurried towards the door when Liam squeezed my arm. But my throat didn't constrict at Liam's grip. If anything, the hold resembled a dog putting its head or paw on its owner. It was nothing like when he'd attacked me the Monday after Evelyn's party.

"Wait," Liam said.

"What?" I asked.

"Please tell me what you're doing in my sister's bedroom. I promise not to judge."

"Please" was the last thing I wanted or needed from him right now. This wasn't the time to be reminded of his softer side. It wasn't like I could just walk away from him. Liam knew where I lived, and besides, he could've approached me at school if he really wanted an answer.

I brushed his arm off. "Why would I ever be honest with you?"

"Because I was honest with you."

"Come again?"

"I said I was sorry and meant it," Liam said.

I furrowed my brow. "Guilty conscience? You don't need to keep apologizing."

"I meant I did something gutsy, and you can do the same."

"You probably apologized so I'd sleep with you," I said.

He shook his head vigorously. "That's not true and you know it. I had no way of knowing you'd forgive me."

"Why do you always fuck me with my face down?" I demanded.

Liam remained silent, rocking his hands back and forth.

"You're ashamed of what's going on between us," I continued.

He forced in a breath. "I didn't realize that was an issue."

"Doesn't matter. I don't care about you enough to be honest."

"Come on." Liam pushed a lock of my hair to the side. Shit. If Liam was going to complain about me using sex to distract him, then he shouldn't have done the same thing. Nothing worse than a hypocrite. "Don't you think I deserve to know whatever it is you're up to if it involves Evelyn?"

The room was spinning so fast I might as well have ingested drugs. Liam's response was the only thing that could've made me tell him about my snooping. I couldn't argue with his comment, even if it *was* emotional blackmail. I would've said the same thing if I were in his position.

"I'll tell you the truth," I said.

Liam shuffled his feet. "Not here, though. I can't take one more second in Evelyn's room."

"Understood."

"No more waffling." Liam locked his door behind us. "We'll both feel better after you tell me what's been going on. Trust me. Secrets can be toxic."

"Do you think I'm crazy?" I asked after explaining my hypothesis.

"No."

"Thanks."

He scratched his neck. "I was the one who found Evelyn and called 911."

Getting shot would've hurt less than what Liam said. Not because I'd ever found a dead family member or friend—I hadn't. But because Liam's comment reminded me of my father. Loss was something I had to live with whether I wanted to or not. Because of course, I so deserved the most morbid life possible.

"Couldn't have been easy," I said.

"Doesn't matter. What's done is done."

I wished Liam knew he didn't have to put on a façade with me. I had nothing to gain by mocking his vulnerability. Plus, he'd already shown his softer side to me when we slept together. Even if he didn't know it.

"Her diary… she was having an affair with a married man," I brought myself to say.

"I could've told you that. She thought she was pregnant."

"How could you possibly know that?"

"I caught her with a pregnancy test."

"Awkward." I suppressed laughter.

"Don't remind me."

"You think someone could've killed her?" I asked.

"I don't know; I was in the shower before I found her."

Damn. I'd really been hoping Liam knew something specific. It would've helped to have proof that I wasn't wasting my time obsessing over Evelyn's death. I could only imagine how most adults might've reacted to my sleuthing. Probably would've said I had too much free time, or that focusing on Evelyn's death was some kind of escapism so I wouldn't have to deal with Dad's death.

"I told you the truth, which means I can go." I was headed toward the door when Liam pulled me up against his body.

He leaned into my ear. "Not so fast."

"Excuse me?"

"Knowing you're capable of scheming is hot." His lips stayed by my ear. "Never thought you were a bad boy."

"One lie isn't the end of the world."

"For you, it might be," he said. Then, "I have to have you."

"Under the same roof as your father?"

"He won't be back for a bit."

"I wouldn't wanna risk anything"

Liam released me. "I can take care of myself, but I appreciate the concern."

I wanted to laugh. Never thought I'd see the day when Liam would risk possible exposure of his sexuality for a quick fuck. Surely, the time we spent together between the sheets couldn't have been that good.

"You really wanna do this right here and now?" I asked.

I had no qualms about being the rational one, no matter that I couldn't get enough of his soft, cotton-like lips. His father could still come home at some point, and I didn't feel like making the local evening news when Mr. Sinclair found Liam and I in bed.

His face drooped. "Not interested anymore?"

"I didn't say that, so don't put words in my mouth."

"My bad."

I licked my lips. "I bet you don't even have condoms and lube."

"You didn't just say that." Liam's eyes narrowed. "Was what you said true, or were you starting a fight as a cover?"

"You're gonna have to be more specific."

"About you always having your head down and you thinking I'm using you for sex."

"I don't think it; I know it," I said.

"I never made any promises to you," Liam frowned.

Promises. What an interesting word. Another example of things left unsaid between us. It was almost as if Liam both wanted more from this arrangement and knew that I deserved something more substantial, even though he could never give it to me. And that meant something. Further evidence that he had more self-awareness than the average teenager—I couldn't imagine Gavin, Mona, and Natalie were capable of such reflection.

"I know," I said.

Liam's shoulders slouched. "I'm not gonna make you stay. I only wanna sleep with people who are interested in me."

I leaned into his face again, lips almost caressing his right ear. "I'm the best offer you've got, because Gavin was right about you. You've never so much as flirted with a girl, let alone used one as a beard before."

"You talk about me with Gavin?"

"Yeah. What are you gonna do about it?"

Liam grunted, then kissed me. His fingers slithered through my hair, grasping every inch of my scalp.

I didn't push him away. And it was only a matter of seconds before we shed clothes.

We didn't hop onto his bed immediately, though. Instead, his head remained buried in my neck while he kissed it. Over. And over. And over again.

Liam tilted his head while we sat in bed after hooking up. "You had your head down again."

"That's how you like it."

He cupped my chin. "I wish things were different, but I wouldn't be involved with someone I wasn't attracted to."

How kind of Liam to give me an ego boost.

"Fantastic," I said.

"I'm serious."

I swallowed down the lump in my throat. Having something beyond sex with Liam might've been great in the alternate universe where we could be a couple. But I knew better. So I didn't allow my mind to wallow in the what-ifs. Liam hadn't done anything to physically harm me since the Monday after Evelyn's party, and that was what mattered.

My gaze shifted away from Liam and landed on the mini fridge at the other end of his bedroom. I pointed to it. "I didn't notice that at first."

"Yeah, it comes in handy sometimes."

I winked. "Got anything exciting in there?"

"Nothing you'd like."

Someone banged on the door and Liam and I exchanged glances.

"Dad?" Liam asked.

"Why the fuck is the door locked?" Mr. Sinclair bellowed.

Liam and I remained silent, eyes on each other.

"You better not be up to anything," Mr. Sinclair continued. "I'd hate to have to teach you a lesson…"

"Don't be ridiculous." Liam placed his hand over my mouth, then brought his free index finger to his lips. "I'm with a girl."

I wanted to scream, but I couldn't. I might as well have returned to the closet—the person I hooked up with shouldn't have been covering my mouth out of fear I would make noise. Thank goodness Liam had locked the door. I couldn't imagine what would've happened if Mr. Sinclair discovered us in bed. His reaction probably would've made Liam's hallway punches look G-rated.

"Great. Carry on." Mr. Sinclair made a clucking noise with his tongue. "Wanted to let you know I'm going out drinking and won't be back 'til late."

"Why did you even come back?" Liam asked.

I might as well have been buried alive. I didn't need physical barriers to feel trapped. I was hostage to this conversation as long as it continued, which Liam should've realized, and should've ended ASAP for that reason. Besides, I couldn't imagine that he actually enjoyed conversing with his father—that would've been like saying sandpaper relaxed people.

"I forgot about a bill I needed to mail," Mr. Sinclair said.

"Please have the bartender call you a cab," Liam said.

"Will do. But I've gotta say one more thing. You don't know how proud I am you finally fucked a girl. Was starting to think you were some loser faggot."

Liam rolled his eyes. "Thanks, Dad."

"I'm serious." Mr. Sinclair coughed. "I never told Evelyn this because she was my favorite, but I hated that she was hanging with that faggot Connor Adams. He always seemed like the world's biggest queer."

My head ached more than someone struggling with a hangover—I'd lost track of the number of times Mr. Sinclair had used "faggot" in the conversation, and I had no fucking clue how much more of it I could take.

Even so, I would've sighed in relief if Liam's hand wasn't over my mouth. His exchange with Mr. Sinclair confirmed my perception of Liam. His difficult home life wasn't just a hypothetical now. He was a victim. Some monsters were made, not born.

"You said you were going out drinking?" Liam asked.

"Right." Mr. Sinclair chuckled, and I felt as if someone had dumped a bucket of ice on me, it was so unnerving. He sounded more menacing than the Wicked Witch of the West. "But I'll leave you twenty dollars on the kitchen counter in case you wanna split a pizza dinner with your fuck buddy. Least you can do after she puts out for you. Who knows? Maybe you'll end up spending the entire evening together."

"Just go!" Liam said.

"Sorry."

The shuffling of Mr. Sinclair's feet grew fainter and fainter until the front door eventually slammed shut.

I shoved Liam's hand off my mouth.

Liam pressed his hands together, jaw quaking. "I'm so sorry."

"Whatever." I hopped out of bed, then grabbed my shorts, boxers, and T-shirt.

"Where are you going?" Liam asked.

"Gotta be anywhere but here."

He wiggled his eyebrows. "Don't you wanna stay and have that pizza?"

I looked at him harder and a jolt of surprise hit me as I realized he was on the verge of tears. Flirting with his eyebrows didn't erase the visceral pain radiating from his eyes. But empathy wasn't a good enough reason to have an obligatory pizza with Liam. And it wasn't only about not knowing what condition Mr. Sinclair would be in when he returned later in the evening. Sharing a meal almost felt like a date, and I couldn't have that. It would've blurred the boundaries of our dynamic, and that would only have confused me. Respect was fair, but I couldn't let myself have a deep emotional connection to someone who'd never be my boyfriend. I just had to protect myself, even if emotions were going to seep to the surface sometimes against my will.

"Do you really think I wanna take your father's money after what he just said?" I slid my boxers up my legs before putting on my shorts and T-shirt. After that, I snatched my flip-flops from the ground in front of Liam's wire hamper, which was so full of clothes it might've fallen over if one more item was added to it.

"I'd be spending his money, not you."

"Don't care about semantics."

Liam glared at me. "It's not my fault my father is a prick."

"That's putting it lightly."

"Where does that leave us?" Liam asked, refusing to look away from me. As if I'd stay if he looked at me intently enough.

I was about to open my locker the following day before lunch as a couple of students and teachers flocked by when my iPhone pinged.

I pulled it out and found one new text from Liam: Can't do this anymore. The arrangement is off, so you'll have to look somewhere else for sex.

Crying at school was social suicide, but tears formed in my eyes.

Liam might not have been the easiest person to deal with, but I never thought he'd break up with me over a text. If I could even call it a breakup. Sleeping together wasn't a substitute for a real relationship, no matter how long our eye contact lingered.

"Something wrong?" Someone asked.

I looked up from my phone. Gavin stood in front of me, scruff no longer on his cheeks.

I wiped my eyes with my free hand. "I'm fine."

He stepped forward. "Let me be here for you. I should've been ages ago."

A few more students darted by while laughter from a nearby clique of girls sitting on the ground erupted through the hallway. Shit. How nice it must've been to be part of that group of girls. I would've given anything to just be happy and not have to worry about my various problems. Like things with Liam being over. Evelyn being dead. Mom always being away from home. Or me being on the outs from my friends.

"You don't have to forgive me. Just tell me what's wrong," Gavin said.

I straightened my collar. "Liam's father almost caught us yesterday."

"Shit. Sorry, man."

"Apparently, his dad's an even bigger homophobe than Liam used to be."

"Not surprised. That kind of behavior doesn't come from nowhere," Gavin said.

"And… Liam just ended whatever was going on between us over text." I flashed my iPhone at Gavin and wiped my eyes again with my free hand.

Gavin didn't speak. Instead, he opened his arms, inviting me in for a hug. I collapsed into Gavin's chest, he patted my back, and I wailed more.

That was the thing about life. Something could be taken away from you when you least expected it, something you hadn't even known you wanted. Liam and I didn't have to be in a serious relationship for the time we'd spent together to mean something.

CHAPTER 8

Overhead lights flickered while I nursed a margarita at the left side of the bar at Chuck's. It was Thursday evening. Mom was out of town on another business trip, so I had an opportunity to test my theory that the older man Evelyn was involved with might come tonight as a tribute to her.

I sipped my margarita, and the mixture of the sweet and bitter flavors jolted my tongue as I looked up. A man sporting a suit sat at the opposite end of the bar. But I had no way of knowing if the person was Evelyn's mystery boyfriend—I needed more context before making an assumption.

The bartender placed a second glass of scotch in front of the guy after he finished his first one. Then, the bartender coughed. "Sorry about your friend, James. Seeing you and Katherine was always nice. Never a dull moment with her."

"Thanks," James mumbled.

The bartender sipped at his white wine, then hid the glass behind the counter. "Although Law is a funny last name. Makes me think of Jude Law."

"Katherine had no relation to Jude Law." James took another swig of scotch.

Katherine Law. The name lingered in my mind for a moment while the door opened and a few patrons flocked into the bar, grabbing a table in the back. Then—duh. I remembered where I'd heard the name before.

I'd walked into a sandwich shop on Main Street a few days before Evelyn's Spring Fling party last May, discovering Evelyn standing in line in front of me.

"Evelyn!" I'd exclaimed.

She'd cocked her head. "Great to see you, Connor. But the name's Katherine Law, so please pretend you don't know me."

"Sure."

The man drank his remaining scotch, then threw a fifty-dollar bill on the bar counter and stood.

"Thanks again, Alan," James said.

Alan chuckled, then took the fifty-dollar bill. "The pleasure is all mine, and I hope to see to you again next week."

"Most definitely," James nodded. "You're the best bartender in town, and the only one I know who drinks on the job."

Alan made a face. "Keep it between us."

James shifted his weight before turning to leave. Someone might as well have ripped out my stomach and wrapped it around my neck. James wasn't just some older man creeping on a teenager. He was Violet Judd's father—I had seen him a couple of times with Violet at school functions.

Damn. Just when the universe couldn't have gotten any more twisted. Sleeping with her best friend's father—a married man—was a new low for Evelyn. No scenario existed where Evelyn would've gotten a happily ever after with James. Not even in the parallel version of Earth where only good things happened.

The only question I had was if James had known Evelyn was pregnant. If so, he'd had a motive for murder.

I sat on a wooden stool in the kitchen the next evening—Mom was still out of town—while the scent of tomato, warm cheese, and other herbs wafted through the air. The delivery person had dropped off a pizza a couple minutes ago, and I was waiting for it to cool off.

The doorbell rang when I was about to bite into my slice. I got the door. I certainly hadn't been anticipating seeing Liam standing on my front porch after his impromptu text the other day, but there he was, spiked hair and all.

His eyes crinkled up in a smile. "Hi, man."

"What are you doing here?" I asked.

"I owe you an apology."

"Can't imagine why. You're Liam Sinclair, and never do anything wrong."

Liam nibbled on the side of his lip. "Fine. I deserved that."

"Go."

He pressed his hands together. "Please let me in."

I could've slammed the door in his face, but it would've wasted time. Not because I wanted to reignite whatever was happening with Liam, but because sometimes letting people say whatever they wanted to say was simpler. If Liam wanted to chat with me, he would, whether it was in the school hallway or at my house on a different day.

I gestured at him and he came inside.

"Make this quick," I said as I sat back on my stool.

Liam scratched the back of his head. "I shouldn't have broken up with you over a text. That was a dick move."

"Breakup isn't the word I'd use. Not like we were dating."

"You know what I meant."

"Save your breath. I know I'm only some piece of ass to you."

"Self-esteem that low?" Liam asked.

I didn't respond. Instead, I bit into the pizza and then sipped my diet ginger ale.

"Never mind—that isn't important," Liam said. "Just know I'd do things differently if I could. But I know I can't..."

A stronger person wouldn't have even heard Liam's apology. But I did, and now a weak question was consuming my mind: I had to know what had caused Liam's change. It wasn't like he'd reversed his opinion about being closeted. He couldn't have. There was a greater chance of pigs flying than of Liam being secure in who he was. One glance at the agony in his eyes was the only thing I needed to see that. Sometimes, a person didn't have to say anything for their truth to be obvious.

"What changed?" I asked.

"Gavin talked to me, and I'm pretty sure he'd beat the shit out of me unless I apologized."

"Sweet. You're doing the right thing because Gavin made you."

He pouted. "I'm really trying."

I raised my eyebrows. "Terrified you won't find anyone else to sleep with?"

A mature person wouldn't have asked that question, yet once again I couldn't help myself. Liam had to like something about me to keep sleeping with me over and over again. And I relished that fact, because it meant I had power in this dynamic. Wanting to feel needed—whether platonically or sexually—was as natural as each day of the week blurring together during a hectic time.

"No," Liam spat.

"Sounds like it to me."

"I don't care if you forgive me. Doing the right thing is what counts."

"Great."

He gripped the sides of his Letterman jacket. "Do you hate me that much?"

"Don't be presumptuous. I never said that."

"You didn't have to. You won't even make eye contact with me."

Satisfaction shouldn't have been my reaction to that, but I loved that Liam was going a little crazy for me, in his own way. Nobody had ever expressed those types of emotions over me before. I'd had zero romantic action with either guys or girls before my encounter with Liam at Evelyn's Spring Fling party.

"Not everything is about you." I took a bite of my second slice of pizza. "I'm just really hungry."

"I see that."

"If you're done, then you can go," I said.

"Wow. Can't wait to get rid of me?"

Interesting. He kept asking me that question in some form or other. If I meant nothing to Liam, he wouldn't have frowned at the possibility of me kicking him out. Because if there was one thing that television shows and movies had taught me about casual flings, it was that romantic feelings sometimes snuck up on a person.

I looked Liam in the eye after devouring the rest of my pizza slice. "You know the rules. If you want something from me, then you're gonna have to ask."

"Not like you'd ever sleep with me again." Liam peeked at the watch on his right wrist. "I should go. I could eat an entire elephant after today's football practice."

"I'd offer you pizza, but you aren't my boyfriend."

"Nope, I'm not."

I gripped a paper towel, then wiped bits of tomato sauce from my lip. "For the record, I forgive you."

"Really?"

"Your father would scare a stoned hippie."

Liam exploded into laughter. "Yeah, he would."

"Hope you have a good evening."

"Bye." Liam darted out of the kitchen, only to return a moment later. "Actually, could I please have a slice of pizza? Or two? I don't feel like cooking or waiting around for takeout after practice."

Again, I took pleasure in something I shouldn't have—Liam looking for an excuse to spend time with me. It was better he made the request that he stay because I couldn't risk being too vulnerable in front of him. If he wanted to continue whatever was going on between us, then he needed to make an effort.

"Sure," I said without hesitation. "Get a plate from the cabinet."

Liam grabbed a plate, then took a few slices of pizza from the box before sitting on the stool next to me.

"Thanks," he said.

"You don't have to thank me for anything—I'm not your boyfriend."

"I'm not an idiot."

"Come again?" I burped after chugging more soda.

"I know you want more than I can offer."

I didn't have a mirror, but I knew the look on my face must've surpassed that of a student discovering all their midterms were canceled. Liam might've been more perceptive than I'd realized.

"I'm used to not getting what I want, so it's fine," I said.

"If it makes you feel better, I'm not in a rush to go home." Liam snatched the diet ginger ale bottle and took several large sips. "Sorry. I should've used a cup."

"Don't worry about it."

"There's something you should know."

"I'm listening." I yawned.

"You're a great guy."

Whether Liam's compliment was because he wanted to sleep with me didn't matter. His remark provided me with another glimpse of his humanity. He didn't have to spend time with me outside of the bedroom, but he was.

We'd never hold hands in public, engage in PDA, or go on a double date—let alone a real date—but I still had this moment, us hanging in my kitchen, and that was something nobody could steal from me.

CHAPTER 9

I opened the door the following afternoon to go for a jog and discovered Liam on my front porch yet again.

I took my earbuds out of my ears, then stuffed them and my iPhone into my pockets. "What are you doing here? You didn't text me."

"I had a moment of serendipity," Liam said.

"Interesting."

Liam gripped the sleeves of his flannel shirt. "Wipe that look off your face. Me knowing a few big words shouldn't shock you."

"I didn't say anything."

"May I please come in?" he asked.

"Sure."

"You're taking a big risk stopping by," I said once he was inside.

"Nice try. I remember you saying your mother wouldn't be home for several days."

"So?"

"Last night was fun," Liam blurted.

"But we didn't have sex."

"Doesn't matter." Liam cupped my chin, making my breathing pick up. One touch might've been harmless, but I didn't know what Liam and I were doing. And that was a problem. Nothing like an ambiguous situation to mess with your head. "You're the only person I've ever had an honest conversation with before."

"That can't be true."

"It is," he said.

I brushed his hand off my chin. "What can I do for you?"

"What makes you think I want something?" Liam asked.

"You always want something when you stop by."

"And that's a bad thing?"

I whipped my head back and forth several times. "Nope. We just gotta be honest with each other. It'll make everything easier."

"I'm not sure what you're getting at."

I lunged forward, then my lips grazed his right ear. "Just us here, so we can be honest."

"Okay..."

"For whatever reason, you're drawn to me."

His face turned redder than Santa Claus. "If you want me to say it, then I will. I wanna sleep with you again."

It was embarrassing, but I squealed. The irony of the situation continued to amaze me. Someone like me shouldn't have had pull over Liam Sinclair. But I did. Him returning to me for subsequent trysts proved that. I was filling a void in his life that nobody else could, and I loved it. My opinion still hadn't changed, though—if something was gonna happen with Liam, then he needed to make the effort. Not me.

"I see," I said.

"What do you say?" he asked.

"We're in the same place we started."

"I don't understand."

"We're never gonna be a real couple."

"Doesn't mean we can't enjoy our time together," Liam said.

"I deserve someone who can offer me the real thing, and it's okay if it's not you. Just gotta be honest with me."

Liam grunted. "Talk a lot about honesty."

"So?"

"You're the one who keeps agreeing to sleep with me."

"And?"

Liam grabbed my hands. "I care about you a lot, Connor."

Interesting. First time he'd called me by my actual name instead of 'man.'

"Actions speak louder than words," I said.

"Seriously going with a cliché?"

"Trite statements sometimes contain the most profound truths."

He continued holding my hands. "I'm not saying we can never go public. I just want some time to process what this means to me."

I nodded at Liam's response. His comment wasn't unreasonable. Liam didn't want me to think he was perfect. He just needed to set his own pace. And that was fine. I couldn't make him do anything he didn't want to.

"Holy shit!" Liam exclaimed about an hour later.

We were on opposite sides of my bed, the comforter covering us from the chest down. The literal distance between us wasn't a big deal. Giving Liam time was one thing, but I also had to protect myself. Protect myself from Liam never accepting himself. Protect myself from never introducing Liam as my boyfriend. Protect myself from the emptiness of how I'd soon be alone in my bed, wondering why I'd chosen passion over substance again.

I wasn't oblivious to the fact that my relationship with Liam resembled a rollercoaster. It'd end one day. Whether because Liam no longer enjoyed the thrill of our hookups or because of me realizing I wanted to be more than someone's secret. And that was fine. The sooner I was able to accept that expiration dates didn't only apply to dairy products, the better off I'd be. It wasn't like Liam felt anything real for me or I could change him. I couldn't, and that was just a fact.

Liam quirked his eyebrows at me. "What are you thinking about?"

"You don't wanna know."

"Okay. I'll take your word for it." Liam plucked a lose eyelash. "But there's something else I wanted to ask you."

"What's up?"

"What do you see in me?" Liam asked.

"Excuse me?"

"I'm being serious."

I forced out a breath. "I see a guy who is trying to be a better person."

"That might be the kindest thing anyone has ever said about me," Liam said. "Wanna know what I see in you?"

I'd never tell Liam this, but a part of me pitied him. My comment couldn't have been the nicest thing someone had ever told him. I was only a booty call, and his teammates, father, and Evelyn should've been supporting him. But no. This was reality, and people often didn't get what they deserved. I gave Liam a cursory smile.

"Sure," I said.

"I see a guy who is confident and doesn't take shit from anyone," Liam said. "And that's sexy as hell. It's also actually why I went off on you the Monday after Evelyn's party."

"I don't understand."

"You own your sexuality, like it's as natural as breathing," Liam said, face resigned. "This isn't easy for me to admit, but I didn't just have internalized homophobia. I was jealous of you."

"I see."

Liam looked down at the comforter. "Hope you don't hate me."

I made eye contact for the first time since we'd hit the sheets today. "Don't be silly."

He wiped at his eyes, which were turning red. "I know I did some fucked-up shit, but all I can do is try and be a better person. I really don't wanna be my father."

I squeezed his hand. "Relax. You aren't your father."

"Thanks," he said.

"There's something I've gotta tell you if we're gonna be honest with each other," I said.

"I'm listening."

"I know who the older man Evelyn was involved with is. It's Violet's father."

Telling Liam about what I knew was fair. And not because I owed him something. I didn't. I just didn't ever want it to come out at the wrong time that I'd known something about Evelyn and hadn't told him. Liam might've been trying to change, but grief still made people do strange things. He might've been only one slip away from the angry, belligerent guy he once was.

"How do you know that?" Liam asked.

"I had a theory that Mr. Judd would still be going to Chuck's as a way to memorialize her, and I'm going back next Thursday to confront him about his affair with Evelyn."

"The fuck you saying?" he asked.

"What if Mr. Judd talked to Evelyn before she died?"

His gaze constricted. "Like Evelyn told him she was pregnant, and he pushed her down the stairs while I was in the shower? Or he stopped by and overheard my conversation with Evelyn before I left her bedroom?"

"Something like that."

Liam didn't respond.

"I'm sure you think I'm crazy, but I don't care," I said. "I've got a bad feeling about Evelyn's death. I owe it to her to investigate every possibility. Letting her murder pass under the radar, if that's what happened… I can't risk that."

"You aren't crazy. Her death was weird."

"Thanks for humoring me."

"But you aren't going alone," Liam interrupted.

"Huh?"

"I'm going with you."

"You don't have to. I'm a big boy, I can take care of myself." I sucked on my thumb. "Wouldn't want anyone to think you were a faggot by association."

He elbowed me. "I can just say you were tutoring me if someone catches us together."

"Perfect. You're a better liar than I realized."

"I've had practice," he said.

I winked. "Should I be concerned?"

"No. But I'm ready for round two if you are."

"Not like I got anything better to do," I said.

Liam scooted to my side of the bed and got on top of me before throwing the bed comforter over us.

"You've gotta admit one thing first," I said.

"And what's that?"

"You're using my return visit to Chuck's as an excuse to spend time with me."

He laughed. "For once, you're absolutely right."

The revelation might not have meant much, but it provided me with some small amount of joy. It let me know that this wasn't a game. That I wasn't wasting my time. It meant we might've had a chance at a real future, if the circumstances were different.

I whistled as Gavin approached me Monday morning in the school parking lot right after I exited my Mercedes.

"You seem happy," he said.

I cocked my head. "Yeah."

"Things with Liam go well?"

"Yeah, they did."

Gavin nudged me. "I'm so thrilled for you, man."

"Thanks." I paused for a beat. "I know you didn't mean anything by it, but please let me handle my own shit next time."

It was a fair response. I didn't need Gavin fighting my battles for me unless I asked him to. It wasn't like I was having a mental health crisis. I just hadn't had a fucking clue about how to deal with Liam after our impromptu "breakup."

"Sure. No problem."

"We actually had a meal together and talked on Friday night."

"How did that make you feel?"

"Happy. For a minute, anyway. Liam will probably be in the closet for the rest of his life." I sighed. "I'm a fucking idiot for hooking up with him."

"No harm in some fun," Gavin reassured me, patting my shoulder. "Anyway, have you thought about ending this tiff thing with us?"

"Just give me some more time."

Gavin scratched the back of his neck. "I'm pretty sure Mona and Natalie would apologize if you gave them an opportunity."

I wouldn't start trouble since Gavin and I were getting along, but I shouldn't have had to give Mona, Natalie, or anyone else anything. If they or anyone else had wronged me, then they could find me and deliver a sincere apology. It wasn't exactly Algebra 2 class.

"And you?" I asked.

"I'm sorry if I was mean about Evelyn. She was only a teenager like us. She deserved an opportunity to be a better person, if that was she wanted."

"Thank you," I said.

The stars and moon illuminated the evening sky while Liam and I sat in my car in Chuck's parking lot on Thursday evening.

Mom had come home and almost immediately left town again for another business trip, and Liam's father probably wouldn't notice that his son wasn't home, so alibis were unnecessary.

Liam rubbed my knee after adjusting his posture in the front passenger seat. "Thanks for being honest with me, man."

"Don't have to thank me."

"Yeah, I do."

"It was the decent thing to do," I said.

Liam snickered. "Don't put on a façade because you're around me. Admit it. You care about me."

"Not like you'd do the same."

"I've never lied to you about my feelings for you," he said.

Feelings. Please. At best, Liam humored me. We'd never have a real teen relationship, and that was okay. Some people weren't meant to have that experience.

My teeth chattered, then I rubbed my hands.

Liam eyed me. "The fuck you doing wearing a T-shirt and shorts?"

"How was I supposed to know it'd get cold?" I asked. "Besides, I can't help that shorts are more comfortable than pants."

Liam took off his Letterman jacket before putting it on me. "Don't say I never did anything for you."

"Whatever."

Though I acted unaffected, surprise still pulsed through my body. Liam might not have been perfect, but he was a nicer person than people realized. If he had really been some heartless jock, then he wouldn't have cared about me being cold. The moment almost reminded me of a scene from a teen program where a guy offered a girl his jacket.

"Look!" Liam exclaimed.

I followed Liam's gaze. Mr. Judd had just walked out of Chuck's.

Liam and I darted out of the car, then accosted Mr. Judd.

"What's going on?" Mr. Judd asked.

"We know you were having an affair with Liam's sister, Evelyn," I said, trying to sound intimidating. "She confessed to everything in her diary, so don't deny it."

Mr. Judd's eyes darted. "Please don't tell anyone."

"Why shouldn't we?" I demanded.

"Because... I... I'm genuinely sorry she died," Mr. Judd said.

"Did you know she was pregnant?" I asked.

Mr. Judd's mouth gaped "What the hell?"

"You knew she was pregnant. You must've argued with her the day she died before pushing her down the stairs," I said.

Liam placed a hand on my shoulder but didn't speak. Didn't have time to analyze his antics when I was close to getting a confession.

Mr. Judd snarled at us. "I couldn't have killed Evelyn if I wanted to."

"The fuck you talking about?" Liam asked.

"I have an alibi for the weekend Evelyn died." Mr. Judd whipped out his iPhone from his jacket pocket. "I was at my cousin's wedding. The rehearsal dinner was Friday, and the actual wedding was Saturday night. Plus, the wedding was in Georgia."

One fact was perfectly clear while Liam and I scrolled through Mr. Judd's photos. He wasn't lying. In addition to timestamps, the photos had dates If I still wanted to prove Evelyn had been murdered, I needed a new suspect.

CHAPTER 10

"Thank you for not thinking I'm crazy," I said.

I was sitting up in bed the evening after confronting Mr. Judd. The comforter covered Liam and I, and again we were on opposite sides of the bed.

He leaned forward. "Why would I think that?"

"Speculating about Evelyn being murdered. It might've been a reach. Wasn't like I had any proof."

Liam sneezed. "There's something I've gotta tell you."

I handed Liam the tissue box from the table next to my bed, but he shook his hand, and I returned the tissues to their spot.

"What's up?" I asked.

"You weren't wrong about my sister being murdered." He made a brief fist. "You just had the wrong suspect."

"Huh?"

"I think my father murdered Evelyn," Liam blurted.

"What are you talking about?"

"I found a cigarette butt by Evelyn's corpse."

I nodded at Liam to continue.

"More specifically, the kind of cigarette my father smokes," he went on. "Marlboro Menthol Lights."

His response was just what I'd wanted to hear—someone might as well have told me summer vacation had arrived nine months early. But it was a crushing realization, too. Having a hunch and actual evidence were two different things, and I didn't know what I could do to make what Liam had just told me okay.

"I'm so sorry, Liam."

"There's more."

"You can tell me anything, babe. I won't judge."

Liam rubbed his scalp but didn't respond. My pulse didn't speed up, though—I couldn't think of anything worse than Liam's father being responsible for Evelyn's death.

Maybe Liam was pissed I'd called him babe. The label might not have been the smartest move. However, some risks were worth taking. Liam and I being alone in my bedroom, he had no reason to retaliate.

Liam chuckled and as if reading my mind said, "Relax. I've got bigger problems than you calling me babe. But don't get any ideas about it becoming a regular basis thing."

"Fair enough."

He lowered his face into his palms. "It's so fucking bad."

I scooted next to him on the bed, then placed a hand on his shoulder. Liam let out a faint sob but didn't push me away.

"We can get through it together," I said.

"I told you I knew Evelyn was pregnant and she was dating an older man, but I didn't tell you when I found that out."

"Why does that matter?"

"I found out before I got in the shower—as in, not long before discovering her body."

"I don't understand."

"We had a big fight about the positive pregnancy test," Liam said.

I held him a little tighter. "Siblings fight all the time. I'm sure Evelyn knew you cared about her."

"I threatened to drag her to the abortion clinic if she didn't go herself."

"I'm sure you were just upset. Besides, life gets messy."

"I wasn't telling her what she should do about her body. I was afraid of what my father would do to her if he found out she was pregnant."

I stroked Liam's hair while my other hand remained on his shoulder. "Didn't your father favor Evelyn?"

"Even that has its limits."

"Was your dad even home when she died?"

"I don't know. Having a big house means keeping to myself whenever possible."

"He wasn't there when the ambulance arrived?" I asked.

"Nope."

"Mind if I ask you a question?"

"Sleeping together means formalities aren't really required."

"Just trying to be polite," I said.

He lifted his gaze from his palms, then looked me in the eye. "I know."

Deep breaths. No harm in asking my question. It wasn't like I wanted to cause Liam harm—emotional or physical. I just couldn't help being concerned—especially if Liam's father was as demented as I suspected.

"Possible your father left the cigarette by Evelyn's body on purpose?" I asked.

"The fuck you implying?" Liam asked.

"Never mind. It was stupid."

"Just say it. Not like anything will offend me at this point."

I squirmed, hesitant to suggest my idea. "Maybe planting the cigarette butt was his way of taunting you. Like saying he'll know you know, but you can't do anything," I said.

"That's a thought."

"Wasn't trying to upset you…"

"I know." Liam kissed me. "You're the opposite of my father. Most generous and incredible person I ever met."

"Don't be silly."

"It's the truth," Liam said. "You were nice to me when nobody else was. Not even Evelyn knew the real me."

No offense to Liam, but he didn't have to thank me for doing the right thing. It was called being a decent person. Besides, I wouldn't have bothered with Liam if I didn't wanna be involved with him. Nobody could make me do something I didn't want to. Not Liam. Not Mom. And not Mona, Natalie, or Gavin, either.

"Happy to help," I said.

He rocked his hands back and forth. "My father might be a twisted motherfucker, but he's not that smart. He can barely get himself to bed after he's been drinking."

Yikes. The visuals in my head were true, then, and I didn't know what to say. My relationship with Mom might not have been perfect, but at least I felt safe at home. That was something everyone deserved. Difficult for people to be decent if they didn't have a solid foundation of parental love and support.

"Could he have overheard your conversation with Evelyn?" I asked.

"His name is on the door where he works," Liam said. "So he can take as many half-days as he wants. He does wills and estate planning, not litigation or criminal law."

"I see."

"Other than his secretary, it's just him at the law firm." Liam cackled. "He never was a team player."

"This problem has an easy solution," I said.

"And what's that?"

"You could ask his secretary if he left work early that day."

"I might not be ready for that answer."

Fair enough. If our roles were reversed, I might've been hesitant to discover whether Mom was guilty of murder. That mantra about knowledge being power was complete bullshit. Information didn't always make people better. It just tormented them—Liam couldn't unlearn whatever answer he got. He had to be sure about whatever he wanted to do next.

I caressed his cheek. "You don't have to do anything you aren't ready for."

"Thanks."

"For what?" I asked.

"Not making me do something I don't wanna do."

I forced in a breath. "I can't make you be something you aren't or do something you aren't ready to."

His eyebrows shot up. "That a jab at me?"

"I was referring to talking to your dad's secretary."

"Still could've meant something else by it."

"What do you mean?"

"Maybe you're not just talking about Tanya. Maybe you're angry about how I'm still in the closet."

"I'm not having this conversation." I looked away while the pattering of outside rain grew louder and louder. Hopefully, Liam and I weren't about to have a fight. I had better things to do on a Friday night.

"Obviously, you still deserve better than what I can give you," Liam said.

Well, at least he was self-aware.

"You're welcome to stay the night if you don't wanna deal with your father." I slid down on my bed, then rested my head on a pillow, back to Liam.

Liam moved toward me before wrapping his arms around me.

I closed my eyes without pushing him away. He cared enough to stay the night, which comforted me. And maybe for a fleeing moment, I could trick myself into thinking my relationship with Liam was real. Something that extended beyond the limits of my bedroom.

"If you have a waffle maker, I can make you waffles in the morning," Liam said.

"Don't hurt yourself."

"Just breakfast."

"Take a joke," I said.

"I'm playing along."

"I know, I know."

The bantering felt like something a real couple would do, too. And I didn't know whether I should laugh or cry about it. The playfulness was cute, but I couldn't get emotionally attached to Liam.

"Waffles are the one thing I know how to cook," Liam said. "Couldn't exactly depend on enabling mother and drunk, homophobic father for breakfast."

"Sorry."

"Stop apologizing," Liam said. "My fucked-up family isn't your fault."

"Still sucks." Not wanting to dwell on something painful to Liam, I attempted to change the subject. "Tell me something about yourself nobody else knows."

"You've gotta promise not to laugh," Liam said after a minute of consideration.

"Sure."

"I'm serious, Connor."

I sighed. "So am I."

"I always wanted to get involved in poetry, but I was afraid my dad would suspect I was gay. So, I got involved in sports."

I almost cried out of sympathy for Liam—Evelyn wasn't the only one who was everywhere and nowhere. Liam's father was fucking up Liam's life even when he wasn't physically around. I was only human, and I couldn't help wondering what Liam's life would've been like if he'd had a more supportive father.

Sunlight glowed through my bedroom curtains the following morning. I stretched and yawned before turning my head. Liam's arms were still wrapped around me, and his eyes were open.

"Morning," he said.

"Hope you don't expect a good morning kiss. I've gotta brush my teeth and use mouthwash ASAP."

"You're adorable when you're nervous."

My bedroom door burst open, revealing my mom standing in the doorway.

"Have you ever heard of knocking, Mom?" I asked, jumping away from Liam.

She giggled. "Not sure how I feel about you having a sleepover."

I wished she'd answered my question. Sleeping with Liam wasn't the only awkward thing she could've encountered. She could've discovered me masturbating. If that happened, I'd probably have to join a witness protection program.

"Fucking bullshit." Liam released me, then moved to the opposite end of the bed. "Don't know what the fuck is wrong with some people." I frowned at him.

"I thought you weren't coming back 'til tonight?" I asked.

"Decided to take an earlier flight," Mom said.

Liam grunted. "Fucking lovely."

Mom rubbed her hands together. "Here's an idea. Why don't I give you two a minute and I'll get breakfast started—seems like we have lots to catch up on."

"No shit," I said.

Mom tried looking Liam in the eye, but he hung his head lower. "Can I at least get a name?"

"None of your fucking business," Liam said.

Mom raised her eyebrows. "I'll go get breakfast started."

She left as fast as she'd appeared, and Liam and I were alone.

So much for Liam's father catching us being the worst thing that could've happened. Liam just hopped out of bed after grabbing his clothes. But his lack of eye contact wasn't the issue. His silence while slipping into his clothes was what made my heart rate increase. If Liam cared about me, then he should've given me something. Something that proved he was more than just a pissed-off guy with no depth. I didn't know what I'd do if Liam ditched breakfast—even he couldn't be that cruel.

CHAPTER 11

Liam craned his neck after he finished getting dressed. "Please make up some excuse about why I can't be at breakfast."

"You're kidding, right?"

"I'm not having breakfast with your mother. No matter how open-minded she is. No offense or anything."

I shrilled at Liam's comment. There was nothing more offensive than people saying "no offense." He knew damn well I'd be offended by his comment. But he obviously didn't care.

"I'm not trying to hurt you, man," Liam said.

I made a clicking noise. "Good to know."

Liam pointed a finger at me. "If you think about it, then it's your fault."

"Excuse me?'

"You should've known your mother was coming home."

"Not my fault she had a moment of serendipity." I threw the comforter back and jumped out of bed. After that, I grabbed my shorts, boxers, and T-shirt.

"Whatever."

"You might not be joining me for breakfast, but you're gonna listen to what I'm gonna say," I said.

Yeah. The fact that I felt like throwing a plate against the wall meant Liam and I were gonna have some words. Not because I wanted to punish him, but because he needed to hear my feelings. If I was going to listen to his father's bullshit, then he could humor me with my parting rant.

"Fun," he said.

"You are a terrible fucking person, Liam Sinclair. Dropping all those F-bombs in front of my mother." I paused for a moment. "What the hell is wrong with you?"

"You already know the answer."

"You didn't have to say anything to her. All you had to do was nothing," I said.

He locked his arms together. "What's done is done."

"There's something else you should know."

"Wonderful."

"My feelings for you weren't real. I was using you for sex to see if I could get with someone who was out of my league."

There was no apology necessary for acting out further. Being a willing participant in this "relationship" with Liam didn't mean I couldn't be upset with him. And right now, I was so upset I wanted to break something. So if I gained superficial pleasure from hurting Liam's feelings, then so be it. Fair was fair. I wouldn't become physically abusive like Liam's father—even I had a line I wouldn't cross. Liam just needed to understand that physical strength wasn't the only metric for pushiness. I could match someone toxic jab for toxic jab. That was what happened when you lost your father at sixteen—you could only depend on yourself.

"Congrats on your victory!" Liam exclaimed.

"This isn't a joke."

"I don't know what you want me to say, man. I can't do anything to change your anger. I should just leave."

"Your father might be a homophobic, abusive drunk, but he isn't stupid," I said.

Liam raised his eyebrows. "Oh, yeah?"

"You deserve to be six-feet under, not Evelyn."

"Ouch. You're gonna make me cry."

I sneered. "Your sister was ten times the person you'll ever be."

"I don't give a fuck about anything anymore," Liam said.

"Don't come crying to me the next time your father beats the shit out of you."

"I won't."

I grinned. "Tell me something. How does it feel knowing everyone hates you? I bet your sports friends are only nice to you because they're afraid of you."

"You don't know what you're talking about."

"I know enough." I straightened my shirt, fixing its creases. "Please don't come find me in a couple of days when you're horny."

"You'd love that, wouldn't you?" Liam asked.

What an asshole. Liam might've been a proficient hookup, but he wasn't the only person I could hook up with. Unlike Liam, I wasn't timid about being gay. If I was really horny, then I could find someone on *Grindr*.

"And don't eye-fuck me when we cross paths in the school hallway," I said.

Liam didn't blink.

"And if I do make eye contact, know how much I fucking hate you," I said.

He gave me a wry smile. "Not gonna beg me to stay or come out of the closet?"

If Liam's comment was his way of demanding help, then he needed to be more specific. I wasn't psychic and couldn't guess his intentions. It didn't even matter if Liam got involved with someone else. He'd never have a successful relationship—platonic or romantic—if he couldn't communicate.

"No point, because you're right. What I said last night *was* a jab at you. But it's fine. You've gotta live your life for yourself, not me."

"You got involved with a closeted guy, so that says more about you than me," Liam said. "Have a thing for emotionally unavailable people?"

"Get real."

"Your way of avoiding getting hurt since you still aren't over your father's death?"

"Don't you dare mention my father," I spat.

"We're done here," Liam said.

I stomped my feet against the ground. "Wait!"

"What the fuck is there left to say?"

"I didn't have my face down to tiptoe around your internalized homophobia. I did it for me," I said.

Gloating might've been cruel, but I almost couldn't contain my glee. I wanted to hammer in the message that physical strength wasn't the only way to win an argument. What I lacked in brute force, I made up for in words. If I wouldn't defend myself, then nobody would.

"The fuck you talking about?" Liam asked.

I cackled so loud I almost gave myself goosebumps. "I was ashamed that I was attracted to someone as *vile* as you."

"It's not like I can come out to my dad—you already know he'd fucking kill me," Liam said. "And I can't file a police report against him for abuse, either. He's the adult, I'm the kid. Plus being a lawyer lends him a certain credibility. So I'm fucked no matter which way I look at my situation."

If Liam's comment was supposed to be another call for help, then he needed to try harder. Nobody could help Liam deal with his shitty home situation unless that was a step he wanted to take—there'd never be a right time to stand up to his father. This conversation was exhausting me more than contemplating the SAT's, college visits, and college applications altogether, but he was making it that way. With Liam, every second might as well have been a decade.

"Whatever," I said.

"Nobody would believe me if I did." Liam put his hands on his hips. "They'll take the word of a respected lawyer any day. Especially in a snotty town like Greenwood."

"Okay."

His Adam's apple bobbed as depression spread across his face. Damn. It was hard to believe I could impact Liam so much. If this were last spring, then I would've never guessed I'd be able to make Liam feel such intense emotions. "Can I please have one last kiss goodbye?" Liam pleaded.

"You want what now?"

"I'm trying to be respectful by asking first."

"We're beyond that," I snapped, fingers tingling. I couldn't believe Liam had asked his question. There was nothing left between us.

"Fine. I don't blame you for hating me."

"I'm serious, Liam. Some compliment isn't gonna get me back into bed."

"Fucking done with this bullshit." Liam slammed the bedroom door behind him, and the sound echoed. I recoiled.

Hard to believe that a relationship that had begun with honest intentions—his apology for his past actions—could end so tragically. But it had. This was real life, not a movie. Not everyone got a happy ending, and Liam would be a distant memory faster than I could count to five.

Mom blew on her coffee while steam seeped from her cup and then took a sip. "I want you to know I'm not mad at you. I was a teenager once, too."

"Thanks." My attention remained on my waffles. "Appreciate it."

"Although it'd be nice to meet Liam sometime. Still can't believe I didn't make the connection that he's Evelyn's twin brother right away." Mom sipped more coffee, then placed the chipped mug down on the table.

"Don't worry about it."

"Do you realize how silly that sounds?" Mom asked. "I'm gonna be concerned about you 'til the day I die."

I shoved my plate to the side. "Please, Mom!"

"Maybe we could have breakfast with him next weekend."

"Not gonna happen," I said.

"Won't know unless you try."

"We ended things before you came downstairs."

"Oh. I'm sorry to hear that. Want me to talk to him?" Mom asked. "Shame for your fun to end."

I didn't know whether I should laugh or die. Mom couldn't have been encouraging me to keep sleeping with Liam. Yet here she was, and here I was, throat constricted. Mom *couldn't* talk to Liam. That conversation wouldn't go anywhere good. Not if Liam couldn't accept or love himself.

"No, thanks," I said.

"I'd be happy to."

"Drop it! This isn't one of your business trips."

Mom gave me a look. "I don't wanna make you uncomfortable, but it might be helpful to vent. These types of things only tend to eat away at you."

"Life can just be so fucked up sometimes." I stood, then grabbed my plate. I threw it across the kitchen before it smacked against the wall. My two waffles dropped on the floor and the plate fragments scattered along the carpet. "Liam is closeted, and I'm a fucking idiot. I knew who he was before getting involved with him, but I slept with him over and over again. I was happy someone who was out of my league wanted me. But that's not the worst part. For a minute, I actually thought we could have a real relationship."

Sweat drenched my back as my chest expanded and contracted. I had no regret about my verbal diarrhea. I might've danced around a lot of what I'd just blabbed to Mom in the past, but my feelings needed to be stated plainly. I'd never have any sanity until I did. My thoughts and emotions mattered, and both Mom and Liam should've realized that like, yesterday.

"I'm sorry," she whispered.

"And I haven't even mentioned Liam's father," I continued, breathing becoming more belabored with each subsequent breath.

"What does Mr. Sinclair have to do with anything?"

"Where should I start? His stupid, violent homophobia is why Liam won't come out. And he physically abuses Liam."

"Ouch."

"I haven't gotten to the best part."

Mom nearly spat out her coffee. "There's more?"

She was about five seconds away from wishing she hadn't asked that question. If I was gonna be honest with Mom about Liam, then I was gonna tell her everything. Including how Mr. Sinclair might've murdered his daughter. I had nothing to lose by being so blunt with her—it wasn't like Liam had sworn me to secrecy about our discovery.

"Liam thinks his father killed Evelyn," I said. "But him finding his father's cigarette butt next to the body isn't enough proof for a murder conviction."

"Why didn't you tell me this sooner?" Mom demanded. "You know I'm only a text or phone call away."

Mom couldn't have been that clueless about why I hadn't included her in more of my life. She would've surpassed the world record for obliviousness.

"Why would I?" I asked.

"Huh?"

"You didn't even acknowledge Dad's birthday a few weeks ago," I said.

"I'm… sorry, sweetie."

"Stop saying you're sorry," I snapped. "I don't need a fucking thing from you or Liam."

Mom rubbed her eye with a napkin from the wooden dispenser on the middle of the table.

"Dad's death taught me how to take care of myself, and that's fine," I said. "We just need to be honest about that."

CHAPTER 12

I shuffled down the lunch line on Monday, already tired even though the week had just started. I was placing a sandwich and bottled water on my tray when the person standing behind me touched my back. I turned and nearly jumped out of my skin. It was Liam.

I hadn't had a lobotomy and the events of Saturday morning were burned into my mind like a CD stuck on the same song. There was no forgetting our messy conversation. I hadn't asked him to come out in front of the school. Just for something to fill up a little of the emptiness rotting through my insides. It wasn't like breakfast would've killed Liam. Mom would've kept his secret. She had nothing to gain by outing him.

Liam gave me a weak smile. "Hi, man."

I remained silent.

He fixed the collar of his flannel shirt with his free hand. "I deserve that."

"No need to chat with me. Remember the rules?" I asked. "Wouldn't want anyone thinking you're a faggot."

"Come on."

"I'm not doing this." I stepped forward in the lunch line while the chattering of numerous voices echoed. There were now only three or four people ahead of me.

"I never meant to insult your mother," Liam said. "It wasn't like I called her a bitch or a cunt or something—I'm not that cruel."

"Could've fooled me."

"We should talk, man."

I moved forward again. It was now my turn at the cash register.

The cashier eyed my sandwich and bottled water. "That'll be five dollars."

"Sure." I grabbed my frayed, leather wallet from my pocket. Except when I opened it, I had to curse under my breath. It was empty.

"Something wrong?" Liam asked.

"I'm so sorry," I said to the cashier. "I thought I had the money, but I guess not."

I left the lunch line and scurried through the cafeteria to a table in back.

Wonderful. I'd forgotten to ask Mom for more money before she left on her latest business trip this morning. For someone who always did their homework during their free periods, I should've been more on top of things.

Whatever. Not eating lunch wasn't the end of the world — I could eat something when I got home from school in three hours. Fasting would be good for me. Maybe I'd feel thinner afterwards.

Someone approached the table and I looked up. Liam handed my lunch tray to me. "Here. Nobody should go without lunch."

I stared, not knowing whether I should accept it or not. "You don't have to do this," I said finally. "I'm not having money problems or anything. Just forgot to ask Mom for more cash, but she can PayPal me funds after school. No big deal."

Liam placed his tray on the table, then sat next to me. "You don't owe me an explanation. Just enjoy your meal. Hangry isn't a good look on you."

"I'll get you the money tomorrow." I bit into my sandwich.

"Don't worry about it. Consider this my good karma."

"You don't have to sit with me."

"You aren't sitting with Mona, Natalie, or Gavin." Liam grabbed a handful of chips from the bag on his tray.

"They're on my shit-list."

"Do I wanna know?" he asked.

"Nope."

Jordon and Evan approached our table with their lunch trays. Then they made eye contact with me.

"What's going on?" Jordon asked.

"Is Liam bothering you, because we'll kick his ass," Evan said.

Liam snickered. "Appreciate the concern, but everything is fine. Now run along and be the airheads you are."

"We weren't talking to you," Evan said.

"Well?" Jordon asked me.

I was tempted to out Liam in front of Jordon and Evan for a split second. Doing so would've meant Liam feeling the same pain I had when he'd skipped Saturday breakfast with Mom and me. Instead, I took in several deep breaths. Revealing Liam's secret to Evan and Jordon would've been too cruel. And not because Liam had paid for my lunch when he didn't have to. Dealing with his drunk, homophobic, asshole father meant Liam had experiences I'd never understand— wounds that would probably remain open until the day Liam died. I wouldn't make his life harder than it needed to be. I also couldn't help being plagued with a small amount of regret. Liam might've been a dick on Saturday, but I'd said some pretty terrible things. Comments I'd have to live with. Comments I hadn't even known I was capable of. Comments I hoped hadn't hurt Liam too much.

"You didn't answer Jordon's question," Evan said through gritted teeth.

"I'm tutoring Liam," I said.

Jordon's eyes bugged out. "Come again?"

Evan held his tray closer to his chest. "You hate each other."

"That's absolutely true—Liam is the scum of the Earth," I said. "And that's why I'm charging him triple my rate."

"Doesn't your mother give you an allowance or some shit?" Evan asked, eyes narrowed in suspicion.

"Still helps to have backup funds."

Jordon surveyed the lunch table before looking back at me. "How come you don't have any textbooks or notebooks out?"

"We were gonna eat first," I said.

"Oh. Okay. Anyway, we'll leave you alone," Jordon trekked away from Liam and me.

Evan followed after Jordon and was soon out of sight.

Liam pressed his hands together. "Thank you."

"Don't thank me for anything. What I said is true. I fucking hate you."

Liam shouldn't have been so presumptuous. I'd never willingly do him a favor. Not if I could avoid it. Too much had transpired between us, and the less I saw of him, the better. There was no point in spending time with Liam if we couldn't be boyfriends, no need to drown on dry land. Being so close—having our secret trysts—but still being unable to actually commit… it was unfair.

"Doubtful. Although the joke is on you," Liam said.

"What are you talking about?" I asked.

"Now we've gotta spend the next forty-something minutes together. Otherwise, Jordon and Evan will know you were lying."

"Huh?"

"I'm afraid so," Liam said.

"Someone might figure out you're gay."

"Don't think so. Not this time." Liam ate the last handful of chips, then tossed the empty bag into the adjacent garbage. "And I've got you to thank for suggesting a perfect cover."

I gave him a pig-like snort. "Who cares."

"Just want us to get back on track."

Someone might as well have just dumped a bucket of ice water on me. Liam couldn't have said what he just had. Even he wasn't that ridiculous.

"Are you even listening to yourself?" I asked.

Liam's elbows slid onto the table before he leaned closer. "Tell me what I've gotta do to get you back in my life."

"You already know what I want..."

"Not that simple," Liam said.

Please. Acknowledging how fucked up our "relationship" had been wasn't enough. Action needed to support talk because I deserved a real future. Not indifferent promises of vague possibilities.

"I'm not gonna give you an ultimatum, because it's not my job to parent you. If you wanna be different, then prove it."

"Not that simple."

"Never is."

CHAPTER 13

I input my locker combination the following morning and my locker clanked open. I rubbed a bead of sweat from my forehead, a small betrayal of the fact that my insides were almost turned upside down. If this were last year, I would've contemplated texting Natalie, Mona, or Gavin before first period.

But no. They still hadn't apologized for their attitude about Evelyn's death. I sighed and stuffed the textbooks and notebooks I'd need for my morning classes into my backpack while students buzzed around the hallway.

"Hi, Connor," called out a voice.

I spun around. Liam was in front of me.

"What'd I do?" I asked.

"Is your self-esteem so low you can't assume someone would just wanna chat with you?" he asked.

"We aren't on speaking terms."

"And that's about to change." Liam pulled me against his body in one swift motion, then kissed me. His hands moved around my head. But I didn't push Liam away—I couldn't win this game until I knew what the rules were. Although I would've been lying if I said I wasn't shocked. Kissing Liam was always great, but I had to have been dreaming. Liam couldn't have been making out with me *in public*—he was the one who had been so conflicted about his sexuality. Yet I wasn't imagining things. The sensation of Liam's lips against mine didn't disappear.

Liam pulled away after a beat, then looped his arms around my neck. "I hope that clears up my feelings."

"Took a big risk with that PDA."

"You're worth it."

"Not trying to be an asshole, but what did you wanna accomplish?"

"I like you a lot, and I don't care who knows it."

Someone could've told me I was going to meet the Pope, and the news would've been more believable than what Liam had just revealed. And not because I was determined to sabotage my own happiness. I wasn't and knew that I deserved joy in my life. It was just close to impossible to believe that the guy who grappled with such serious demons was capable of such a transformation in a short amount of time.

"What if word gets back to your dad?" I asked. "He'd kill you if he ever found out about this."

"Doesn't matter."

I must've been having a fever dream. This kind of honesty from Liam wasn't possible, yet I was still standing in the hallway when I opened my eyes after blinking hard several times.

"I'm glad you're okay with yourself, but I hope you didn't come out of the closet only for me," I said.

He licked his lips. "No, I did it for myself as much as I did it for us. This noose keeps getting tighter and tighter."

"Happy for you."

Liam's eyes sparkled, mirroring the sunlight trickling into the hallway from a nearby window. "Where does this leave us?"

"Excuse me?"

"I want you to be more than my fuck-buddy."

I lifted my brow. "What are you saying?"

"I want you to be my boyfriend."

Boyfriend.

I couldn't deny that the word had the same appeal as my birthday or Christmas. I had a chance at the one thing I'd been aching for but never thought Liam could give me—a real relationship. An opportunity to hold hands, have PDA; a chance to go on a real date, and not pretend Liam was a friend when running into an acquaintance.

I almost cried.

"Really?"

"The fuck you asking that for?" Liam demanded. "I'm giving you what you want."

"I need a stiff drink."

"I have a flask in the glove compartment of my car," Liam said.

"Are you kidding?"

He swallowed. "Nope."

"There are still things we've gotta figure out," I said.

He looked away. "I don't wanna discuss Evelyn right now."

"Understood."

Liam's eyes darted back to mine and he nudged my shoulder. "You should be happier."

"I was unfair to you," I said. "I shouldn't have said those harsh things. You deserve better than me."

"You were having a moment—it's called being a teenager."

"I was gonna out you to Evan and Jordon yesterday because I wanted you to feel as bad as I did."

The scorching sensation consuming my stomach was worth telling him that. If Liam and I were gonna be a real couple, then there couldn't be any secrets between us. Not because I expected our relationship to be perfect, but because having more open communication would help us avoid future problems A relationship needed to involve more than taking the temperature of the dynamic.

"You didn't," Liam said.

"But I wanted to."

"Not giving into impulses shows you're a good person."

I buried my face in my hands. "You don't hate me?"

"Nope. Although I'm done talking."

Liam grabbed my hand before leading me down the hallway.

Everyone was focused on us. Except nobody booed or made a snide comment. Liam had the one thing he'd always wanted. Acceptance. Someone should've taken a picture of the moment. Liam deserved to feel this good about himself always.

Several hours later, I bumped into Natalie, Mona, and Gavin on the way to lunch.

Gavin eyed me. "Hi, man."

"The whole school is talking about you and Liam," Natalie said.

Mona flipped her hair over her shoulders. "All good things, though."

"Fantastic," I said.

Mona smiled. "You deserve this."

"Thanks," I murmured.

Natalie tightened her backpack strap. "We should talk."

"I'd love that, but Liam and I are gonna have lunch together." I rubbed the back of my neck while my heart pounded faster and louder. "He wants me to sit with him and the football team."

Gavin rubbed the scruff on his right cheek. "Everything okay? I don't think they'll give you a hard time."

"It's not that," I said.

"Then what?" Gavin asked.

I grinned, excitement happiness radiating through my body. "Just can't believe I'm getting everything I wanted."

Gavin pinched my shoulder. "Live in the moment and take some deep breaths."

When Gavin was right, he was right. The most anxiety-inducing situations sometimes ended up being the easiest. No point in inventing drama before it happened. Lunch with Liam's football friends would either go well or it wouldn't. I wouldn't turn into the stereotypical neurotic fool when it came to dating—especially when Liam and I still needed to figure out whether his father had murdered Evelyn.

"Here." Mom handed me a cup of hot chocolate while we were in the kitchen before school.

"Thanks."

"Don't have to thank me for anything. I'm your mother."

"Nice of you to catch a flight home for twenty-four hours."

"I need to start being more involved in your life," Mom said.

"Doesn't matter."

"It absolutely does."

I took a large sip of my hot chocolate, then placed my mug on the kitchen counter. "You must be pissed Liam is my official boyfriend after what I told you last Saturday."

"I'm not gonna judge you when I've been so absent from your life." Mom gripped a chunk of her hair. "And I want you to know I meant what I said. I'm not gonna meddle in Liam's life, no matter how much I might loathe his father's actions. It would only make the situation worse."

"Thanks."

"Liam is welcome to sleepover in your bedroom anytime if he needs to get away from his father."

Frost might've been tinting the kitchen window—the temperatures had dipped below freezing last night—but I wouldn't fret. Having this small conversation with Mom proved that life could pivot. Maybe, just maybe, my luck was improving. Having false hope was better than no hope—everyone deserved a little happiness.

CHAPTER 14

I shuffled through the hallway the following morning on the way to third period and ran into Natalie, Mona, and Gavin.

"Hi, man." Gavin adjusted the baseball cap that sat backwards on his head. I would've criticized him for wearing it like that if it weren't for his age. Long as you were younger than your mid-twenties, you could get away with wearing your baseball cap the wrong way without looking like a douchebag. "Ready to have that talk?"

"Sure. We've got plenty of time before the warning bell," I said.

We all stepped into an empty adjacent hallway.

"We're sorry Evelyn died," Mona said. "She didn't deserve what happened to her, and she could've changed if she wanted to."

Natalie tucked a lock of hair behind her ear. "Mona's right. We don't need to punish her for what she did to us, and we should all move on with our lives."

"I'm also sorry we were gonna end our friendship with her that Friday afternoon," Mona said. "Maybe you were right about there being extenuating factors, Connor."

I didn't speak.

Gavin chuckled. "Something wrong, man?"

I let out a nervous laugh. "What gave it away?"

"Please tell us you accept our apologies—there's nothing else we can say," Mona said.

"It's not that," I said.

"Then what?" Natalie asked.

The lump in my throat felt like it was choking me. Trusting Natalie, Mona, and Gavin with such a big secret was risky. But I didn't have a choice. And not because I believed my friends were perfect—I didn't. There was just something liberating about the idea of discussing the Evelyn situation with someone other than Liam. It wasn't like I could talk too much with Mom about Evelyn's death. I didn't wanna give her a reason to worry. Being closer to Mom would've been nice, but not if it made her become a helicopter parent. Too much hovering was the last thing I needed. I was still a teen and enjoyed having independence.

I put my hands in my pockets. "I'm gonna tell you guys something, but you can't tell anyone. It's about Evelyn's death."

They all nodded.

"Liam and I think she was murdered," I revealed. "Evelyn was having an affair with an older man—Violet Judd's father."

Squeaky footsteps echoed, and I peeked at the turn in the hallway. Nobody was there. Creepy. I could've sworn someone had almost walked down the hall. Almost as if somebody had been eavesdropping on our conversation.

"You were saying?" Gavin asked.

I chewed on the inside of my lip. "Evelyn was pregnant at the time of her death."

Mona played with a strand of hair. "You don't think Violet's father killed Evelyn, do you?"

"Mr. Judd isn't the problem. He has an alibi," I said.

"Then what?" Natalie asked.

"Mr. Sinclair," I mumbled.

Gavin gave me a look. "What do you mean?"

"He might've pushed Evelyn down the stairs. Liam found one of his father's cigarette butts by Emily's body," I said.

Mona massaged her lip, smearing her lipstick, then shook her head as she stared at her lipstick-covered finger. "Are you serious?"

"Liam has no way of knowing the truth for sure because he was in the shower, but we're pretty sure," I said.

Natalie gripped her neck. "What more do you need?"

"Liam and I plan on talking to Mr. Sinclair's secretary," I said. "She can vouch for whether or not Mr. Sinclair left work early that Friday."

"I still don't understand how he would've had a motive to kill Evelyn." Gavin fixed his basketball shorts.

"Liam and Evelyn had a big fight before he took a shower—he wanted Evelyn to get an abortion," I said. "Something about being afraid of how their father would react to Evelyn's pregnancy. So maybe he overhead the conversation and waited for Liam to leave Evelyn's bedroom."

Natalie rolled up her sleeves. "No offense, but those are big assumptions."

"The cigarette butt is the big tell," Mona said.

Mona was right. Liam had no reason to lie to me about finding his father's cigarette butt at the scene of his sister's death. Liam and I had been through so much in such a short amount of time.

"I wasn't joking about you guys not telling anyone." My arm hairs rose. "I don't know what Liam's father would do if he knew Liam suspected him of killing Evelyn."

"Understood," Gavin said.

"What about Mr. Sinclair's… less-than-tolerant attitudes?" Natalie asked. "Aren't you two afraid he'll find out about your relationship?"

Mona jabbed Natalie's shoulder.

"I'm not trying to be a bitch," Natalie continued. "Just being honest. I'd hate to see your newfound happiness ruined."

"I don't think Liam cares at this point," I said.

The bell rang, then a group of students and several teachers burst into the hallway while Natalie, Mona, Liam, and I exchanged glances.

"Thank you for accepting our apologies," Mona said.

Mona didn't have to thank me for dropping our dispute. If I wanted to punish her and the others more, I would've. But there was no time for petty grievances when I was trying to discover the truth about whether Mr. Sinclair had pushed Evelyn down the stairs.

I waved my hand. "Please. All that crap is in the past. It doesn't matter."

Mona suddenly squealed at me. "Who knows? Maybe you, Liam, Gavin, and I could go on a double date at some point."

Her enthusiasm made my pulse audible in my ears. My relationship with Liam became realer with each passing second. Having a double date was the type of thing "normal" teens did. But Liam and I hadn't even had a real date yet…

"Only after Liam and I have our first date," I said.

"It'll happen. If I know Liam, then he's probably working up the courage to ask you," Gavin said.

"We should have a group hug," Mona said.

"Excellent idea," Natalie parroted.

We hugged each other. I was between Gavin and Mona, and an elephant might as well have been sitting on me. I almost couldn't breathe. Although the near suffocation might've been a good thing. The moment made me aware that I was capable of feeling happiness. So the discomfort was worth it, just this once. Anything that meant I was alive and human was a good thing. High school would've been lonely without any friends.

I caressed Liam's knee while we sat in the front of his car on Saturday night. "Just remember that we're gonna get an answer one way or another."

"I know," Liam said.

"Thank goodness you're more than a pretty face, because I don't know what we would've done if you hadn't remembered your dad's secretary goes to Lindsay's every Saturday."

Lindsay's. The name was an interesting choice for a sushi place. Although I'd refrain from passing judgment. Until Liam and I chatted with his father's secretary, nothing else mattered.

"I'll take that as a compliment," Liam said.

"Trust me. I'd let you know if I had a problem with you." I grabbed my hot chocolate from the cup holder and took a sip. The combination of the warm sweet and chocolate flavors jolted my taste buds while I closed my eyes for a second. If I was gonna wear shorts in forty-degree weather, then I needed a way to stay warm. I'd never give up wearing shorts. They were more comfortable than pants. I'd always be one of those guys who sported them even when there was a foot of snow on the ground.

"Good." I flashed the cup at Liam. "Thanks again for this."

Liam snickered. "I wasn't about to give you my Letterman jacket again. It's fucking freezing."

"Good to know you care, babe." I placed my drink back in the cup holder while a nearby car alarm blared for a good ten or fifteen seconds.

He coughed. "There's a thing I wanted to ask you."

"And what's that?"

"It's not a big deal…"

"I promise not to laugh."

Liam returned his focus to me. "I was wondering if you'd wanna go out on a date next weekend."

So, he was really making that move.

"Big step. Ready for it?" I asked, feeling jittery myself.

"Absolutely."

"Good. And… yes. I'd love to go out on a date with you."

Liam didn't speak. His gaze was focused on the woman who'd just strutted out of Lindsay's. She wore a matching purple blazer and skirt, and a gust of wind was whipping her bob haircut into her face.

"Showtime," Liam said.

Liam and I exited the car, then cornered Katie as she approached a station wagon with peeling paint on the right side.

"Can I help you with something?" Katie demanded.

"I'm Liam—Joseph Sinclair's son," Liam stammered.

"I know who you are," Katie said. "I'm sorry for your sister's death."

"Do you remember the day she died?" Liam asked.

"Yes, I had a hair appointment that day," Katie said. "Why?"

"Did my father slip out of work early that day?" Liam asked. "Anything you could tell us might be helpful."

"I don't like what you're implying," Katie said, eyes growing guarded.

Yikes. Maybe Liam's father didn't have the perfect reputation that he thought he did. Both the tone and inflection in Katie's voice told me everything I needed to know.

"Answer the question," Liam said.

"Yeah, he left work early that day." Katie grabbed her car key from her blazer pocket, and her car beeped before the locks jumped up.

"Probably shouldn't tell my father about this conversation," Liam said.

I was glad Liam had thought to say it. I didn't know what we would do if Mr. Sinclair discovered our snooping.

"I'm not stupid. Getting on his bad side is the last thing I want." Katie got in the car, closed the door, then started the ignition before barreling out of the parking lot.

"If my father actually killed my sister, then I don't know what I'm gonna fucking do," Liam said a moment later.

He collapsed into me while I patted his back and he sobbed into my chest.

Shit. Sometimes, I didn't wanna be right. Knowledge wasn't always power. Now that Liam truly suspected his father had murdered his sister, his head must've been ready to burst. And I didn't know what Liam and I were gonna do with this truth. That kind of violence—a father killing his own daughter—was personal and cut deeper than any weapon could've.

CHAPTER 15

The temperatures had returned to the seventies by Wednesday, so I sat at one of the wooden tables in front of my high school's main entrance finishing some Algebra 2 homework.

Evan and Jordon approached me, then sat down.

Jordon threw his backpack on the table. "Hi, man."

"Something wrong?" I asked.

"Everything is fine. Man, you need to worry less," Evan said.

I smiled at them. "Cool. What can I do for you?"

"Your relationship with Liam is great," Jordon said.

I gave them a mock scowl. "Thanks, I think."

"We're serious," Evan said. "We've never seen Liam so happy before. And having you in his life has also been good for his football game. He's become less of a diva and more of a team player on the field."

I closed my textbook. "You didn't have to track me down to tell me that."

"Yeah, we did," Evan said. "Liam never knew real happiness before you."

My insides filled with more joy than a prisoner must've felt being released on parole. It was good to know I had an impact on Liam's life. I would've hated to think our relationship had been for nothing.

I let out a small laugh. "I'm his boyfriend, not a miracle worker. If Liam changed, then he did it for himself."

"You're a positive influence on his life." Jordon removed his baseball cap for a second, then ran his fingers through his hair. "So, please let us know if Liam's dad ever gives you shit."

No offense to Jordon, but his words were meaningless. Removing Mr. Sinclair from Liam's life would take more than a couple of teenagers. If the universe was on Liam's side, then his toxic home situation would resolve itself. It just had to. Liam would never be at peace until he freed himself of his father once and for all.

"Will do. But I don't wanna meddle in Liam's life." I tapped my pencil against the table. "Although maybe he should consider emancipation if his situation is that dire."

"There's always jury nullification," Evan said.

Jordon's eyes bulged. "What now?"

"It's when someone commits a crime, but the jury votes not guilty anyway. Like if someone killed their abusive spouse in defense," Evan said.

Jordon made a tsk-tsk sound. "And you know this information how?"

"I watch *Law and Order* reruns with my mom."

Jordon tugged at his hoodie strings. "Hope you aren't suggesting we kill Mr. Sinclair?"

"Forget it. It was a joke," Evan said. "Clearly not as funny as I thought."

"No shit," Jordon said.

"Relax. Not like I wanna hurt Mr. Sinclair for real."

I hummed but didn't respond to Evan and Jordon's banter. The thought that had popped into my head wasn't a nice one. So, I'd keep it to myself. I didn't need people looking at me like I had fifty eyes because I wouldn't have blamed Evan if he was serious. Forgiveness didn't always entail healing, and that looked to be the case with Liam's fucked up home situation. More violence was sometimes the only way to end violence—there was a difference between what was morally and legally right.

I stood next to Mona in one of the local boutique shops on Main Street the following afternoon.

Mona waved a salmon-colored strapless dress at me. "What about this?"

"No comment," I said.

She huffed in exasperation. "Don't be crazy. I brought you here because I wanted your expert opinion. Every girl needs a gay best friend."

"Great to know I'm good for something," I said.

"I promise I won't be angry if your opinion offends me."

"That's what people always say right before they get pissed off."

"Not this time. My anniversary date with Gavin is a big deal, and I need to look sexy as hell."

I covered my ears. "Don't make me go deaf."

"Don't be a prude," Mona said. "You've probably hooked up with Liam a million times."

"Mona!" I exclaimed.

Mona held the dress closer to her body. "Enough stalling. Give me your honest opinion."

"I hate it. The color is hideous." I picked another strapless dress off the rack, then dumped it into Mona's arms. "Here."

"Why this?"

"You wear a lot of hot pink and light purple lipstick, which would match this hot pink dress better than that atrocious dress you picked," I said.

"Might have a point."

Thank goodness Mona didn't decide to fight my opinion—I didn't know what I would've done if she had. Getting back to being friends meant we didn't need any drama for a while. Sometimes, one false move was the only thing needed to make a situation implode.

I towered over Mona. "Admit it. I'm always right."

"Don't get cocky."

"This has been great, though. Kind of like old times."

Mona returned the salmon-colored dress back to the rack before studying the one I'd picked out. "Excited for your date with Liam?"

"Terrified," I said.

Mona met my eyes. "Why?"

"We're going ice skating for our first date," I said. "Something about how he used to love it as a kid but picked football and lacrosse because he thought those were more masculine sports than ice hockey."

"Poor guy."

"I'm probably gonna fall flat on my ass," I said.

She giggled. "Don't be close-minded. Maybe ice skating will surprise you like Liam did. Or maybe you're right, and it'll be awful. But I guarantee you one thing. If you go into your first date with that attitude, you'll leave disappointed."

Not rolling my eyes at Mona took all the energy I had. Admitting she was right and accepting she was right were two different things. Having Liam take our relationship public was great, but I didn't understand why we couldn't just go out to dinner or to the movies—like a normal first date.

I stood at the entrance to the rink Saturday evening. Liam was already gracefully moving across the ice, swooping around the circumference with sure, steady strides.

Sweat dripped down my forehead and I felt like I needed one of the famous soap opera slaps. I knew I was being bratty. Liam and I could always go out to dinner for our second date, and I should've been ecstatic I had a real boyfriend. But I was human and couldn't help the trepidation soaring through my body.

Liam skated toward me. "Something wrong?"

"It's gonna sound stupid."

"Try me."

"You'll laugh."

Liam's arms coiled around my shoulders, the fruity and sweet scent of whatever aftershave he used filling my nose before he picked me up, making my skin prickle. "It's me you're talking to."

"I'm afraid of hurting myself. Or worse, being a total and complete ditz."

"I see."

"You wanna laugh, don't you?" I asked, eyes on the ground.

"Didn't say a word."

"Sorry I've got a stick up my ass."

"I'll be right here to catch you if you fall, but you've gotta trust me," Liam said.

My heart skipped a beat. Knowing Liam had my back was nice. If it were me, I might've teased someone for being clumsy. Yet Liam hadn't mocked me. So, in a small way, I felt closer to Liam. Not having to hide something about myself—even something as mundane as being uncoordinated—was great.

"Okay," I forced out.

Liam moved a few yards back onto the rink, then gestured for me to come out.

I skated towards Liam after several additional breaths, and when I approached him, he held my hands.

Liam resumed his skating, moving the same way he had before, and I was able to catch up to him without panting or sweating.

The pattern repeated over and over until Liam and I were on opposite ends of the rink—which was only slightly smaller than my high school's football field. But just like how I'd let myself go following Liam across the ice, I'd banish any doubt from my mind about the return trip to his side.

In the same way that I brought out a different side of Liam—he might not ever have accepted himself without meeting me—he also made me bolder. Before Liam, I would've kicked my feet and stormed away from someone at the suggestion of doing something new. But not now. Not when I was getting everything I wanted.

Liam's eyebrows arched. "Don't hurt yourself with all that thinking."

"I'll be fine," I said.

"Great." He stretched his arms and legs. "Anyway, I was thinking we could go to Starbucks and get hot chocolates after this."

Thank goodness there was a second part to this date. Refreshments were the perfect next step to an evening that hadn't lived up to the nightmare I'd concocted in my head. Gavin had been right—living in the moment was best if I didn't want to drive myself crazy.

"Really?" I asked.

"I had a sip of the hot chocolate I bought you the day we tried to talk with Katie, and it wasn't bad," Liam said. "Starbucks is still a fucking rip-off, though."

"Fair enough."

Liam lightly bopped my nose. "But you're worth it."

"Thanks."

"I'm serious, Connor. I don't know what I'd do if anything ever ruined our relationship."

The old me might've joked about Liam spending too much time with me—I had the monopoly on being cynical. But I couldn't. The only thing I was feeling was sorrow. I wondered if Liam's battered state meant he believed he didn't deserve to be happy, and that the universe would take a wrecking ball to our relationship.

"Let's pray that never happens," I said.

He returned my smile with one of his own. "Agreed."

CHAPTER 16

Liam greeted me with a quick kiss in the school hallway the following Thursday morning.

"Glad to run into you. There's something I wanna talk about," I said.

"Hope it isn't bad."

"Nope. The opposite, in fact."

"Great."

"My mom is gonna be home for forty-eight hours starting tomorrow night." I picked a loose eyelash irritating my right eye. "She knows we've been spending a lot of time together and wanted have a redo of the breakfast we never had."

"I see." Liam removed his water bottle from his backpack and took a good swig of water before screwing the cap back on tight.

"No pressure. I can invent an excuse if you don't wanna do this."

His arms dropped to his sides after he put the water bottle back. "I thought things were going well."

"They are."

The side entrance door opened and a teacher sporting a leather jacket entered the building. Wind swooshed through the hallway, ruffling my hair. But messy hair was the least of my concerns right now. I needed an answer from Liam about what he wanted. It seemed plausible that he would agree to the breakfast. We'd been through so much in a short amount of time—one meal with Mom shouldn't have been a big deal.

"Then let's absolutely fucking do this," Liam said. "Coach switched Saturday practice to Sunday, so I can do breakfast Saturday morning."

"Perfect." I kissed Liam, this time letting the embrace last slightly longer than the one moments earlier.

"I'll go to Starbucks and pick-up breakfast on the way," Liam said. "That'll take the pressure of cooking off your mom."

I would've smiled at Liam, but I didn't wanna make a big deal out of his remark. Doing something without being asked to made Liam an even more perfect boyfriend. Relationships were about effort, and I didn't wanna be the person in the relationship who cared more. Not after Dad's death. Not when I couldn't afford to lose another piece of myself.

"Sounds good," I said.

He scratched his right shoulder. "If I recall, you like their hot chocolate?"

"If you don't know I like hot chocolate, then our relationship might be doomed."

"I'm kidding."

"I know," I said.

Gavin and I sat at a table at the mall's food court the following day after school, having ice cream.

"Thanks for your help." He finished the last scoop of his ice cream, then snatched a napkin from the metal dispenser on the middle of the table. "I don't know what I would've done without you, man."

"No problem." I took another bite of my soft serve vanilla ice cream. Nothing like a refreshing treat on an 80-degree day. "Part of the job description of being a best friend."

"I hope it's enough."

I peeked at the bag under our table, then returned my attention to Gavin. "She'll love it. You need to take your own advice."

"What are you talking about?" he asked.

"Live in the moment."

"Ah. You might have a point. And Mona *has* been too busy to replace her iPhone case."

"Simple gestures are sometimes enough—even if this is your two-year anniversary."

"I should also be thanking you for taking Mona shopping last week." He took his hoodie off and tucked it under his right armpit. "She didn't say it outright, but I'm sure she appreciated you taking the time for her."

I shook my head at him. "No more formalities. I'm not gonna wake up tomorrow and change my mind about wanting to be friends with you guys."

I had nothing to gain by cutting Mona, Natalie, and Gavin from my life. They could make mistakes—like being overly judgmental of Evelyn—just like Evelyn had made some mistakes when she was alive. We were still kids, and it would've been naïve to think we couldn't evolve if we wanted to. Nothing was certain in life except death— Evelyn was proof of that fact.

Gavin grabbed a napkin from the metal dispenser next to us and started shredding it into pieces. "Good to know."

"I'm serious, Gavin."

"How are things with Liam?" he asked abruptly.

I fixed my posture. My back had started aching. "Fine. He's coming by tomorrow morning for breakfast. My mom is gonna be there, too."

"Nervous?"

"It'll be a trip to Starbucks compared to being around his father."

"You should be proud of yourself. You're dating one of the most popular guys in school," Gavin said. "Not something most people can say."

"Didn't happen exactly like that." I dug at the sides of my cup, scraping off the last bit of ice cream and scarfing it down in a matter of seconds. Then I grabbed Gavin's cup and spoon and tossed our garbage into the bin next to us.

"Good aim," Gavin said.

"There's something I need to tell you," I said.

"I'm listening."

"Liam hasn't done anything with the information that his dad was probably at home when Evelyn died."

"It's his dad, not yours."

My teeth ground together. "I don't like Liam being alone in the house with that guy. Not even for a second."

Gavin shoved his hoodie into the bag holding the iPhone case he'd bought for Mona. "If you're really this concerned about Liam, then you need to talk with him."

Gavin made a good point. If I had something to say about Mr. Sinclair's involvement with Evelyn's death, then I needed to do something about it. Doing nothing only ensured that the situation wouldn't change.

Liam chuckled. "You never told me your dad was on the football team in high school."

Mom, Liam, and I sat at the dining room table, chowing down on the Starbucks breakfast Liam had purchased on the way to my house.

"I didn't know," I said.

"Don't lie to your boyfriend." Mom broke off a piece of apple fritter before sipping more of her coffee. "You knew. Probably just didn't care."

"Or I wasn't paying attention," I pouted.

"Yup," Mom said.

Liam took a napkin from his paper bag, then wiped at the powdered sugar coating his lips. "I need to apologize for my behavior."

"What are you talking about?" Mom asked.

"I shouldn't have skipped out on a breakfast, and I shouldn't have dropped all those F-bombs in front of you." Liam gulped down the rest of his hot chocolate before crushing the cup.

Color me impressed. I hadn't mentioned the issue to Liam, but I'd hoped he'd consider apologizing to Mom. Not because what he'd done was the worst thing in the world, but because there couldn't be any awkwardness between Liam and Mom if I wanted my relationship with Liam to succeed.

"I don't give a fuck," Mom said. "It's over and done with."

Thank goodness Mom was so easygoing. Her forgiveness was better than a dentist's checkup without news you had cavities. Mom could've been petty if she wanted to, but she wasn't.

My mind couldn't help wandering, though. I wondered if Liam's home life wasn't the only motivation for Mom's forgiveness. More specifically, if the pain from losing Dad was still palpable for her, and she didn't want me to experience those same emotions. The type of feelings that made someone not care whether they woke up in the morning.

"Thanks," Liam said.

"But there's one thing we should discuss." Mom grabbed a hair tie from the table, ran her fingers through her hair, then pulled it into a ponytail. "If you two are sleeping together, then you've gotta practice safe sex."

I banged my fist against the table. "Mom!"

"Don't mistake my open-mindedness for cluelessness," Mom said. "I haven't forgotten about walking in on you two."

I buried my head in my lap. "Kill me now."

"Don't be so dramatic," Mom said.

"Relax, Connor." Liam took another bite of his breakfast sandwich. "You don't know how great having a normal problem is."

If Liam could rationalize Mom chatting with us about sex, then good for him. But not me. What happened between us in my bedroom was nobody's business but ours. Liam might've no longer been closeted, but the most intimate details of our relationship were just for us. They were ours, and ours only.

CHAPTER 17

I was lying at the edge of my bed several evenings later while Liam once again sported a goofy grin at the opposite end of the mattress, both of us stretched out under the comforter. Sweat dripped down our faces as we caught our breath.

"I don't know if I should be offended or laugh," he said.

"About what?"

"You always move away from me the second we finish."

I bit my nail. "I can't help it."

"Still uncomfortable around me?"

I wished he hadn't asked. We'd made significant progress in our relationship and didn't need to continue dwelling on past drama. If I needed to discuss it, I would. But until then, our baggage didn't matter. If I wanted to believe a fresh start was possible, then I actually had to live the new beginning.

I tilted my head. "We both know I don't do anything I don't want to."

"Then what gives?"

"You aren't the problem, your father is."

His lips curled. "No offense, but he isn't appropriate bedroom conversation."

"We need to put an end to this one way or another," I said.

"My father isn't the nicest person..."

"No shit."

"Did you have something in mind?"

"You never told me what you did with the cigarette butt," I said.

I had no misgivings about bringing up Mr. Sinclair potentially being a murderer. It was an issue that needed discussing. Ignoring it wouldn't make the matter vanish. Nothing would. Mr. Sinclair was a monster, and people like him thrived on their ugliness going unchecked.

"I grabbed a tissue, picked it up, and put it in a bag before calling 911." He eyed me. "But why does that matter? One cigarette isn't enough for a murder conviction."

"You're right. It isn't."

"Then what?" Liam demanded.

My pulse hammered in my ears. "My mother has a gun. She bought it after my father died when she was going through a phase."

"Okay?"

"It's in her safe, and she trusted me with the combination."

He snorted. "For real?"

"Something about wanting me to have protection in case of emergencies."

Liam scooted next to me, and I didn't recoil. "Good thing I'm around. Not sure I like the idea of you handling a gun."

Please. I wasn't a little kid. I wasn't dumb enough to play with the gun after a night of drinking. No, thanks. Didn't feel like making the local evening news.

"We took a couple of classes," I said.

"That's better than nothing," Liam said. "But what does that have to do with my father murdering Evelyn?"

"It's obvious we're never gonna have any concrete proof of what he did."

Liam nodded.

"But we could record a confession and use that to pressure him to go to the police."

"Don't think so."

"Think about it. It'd be two against one."

"That's… a very dangerous game," Liam said, brow furrowing.

"Don't you want justice for Evelyn's death?"

"Not if it means risking your life." He cupped my chin, sending chills up my back—I'd never get used to how I'd transformed from the kid who'd never kissed a guy or girl into the person who thought romantic displays of affection were as natural as needing oxygen to survive. "Important to know when something isn't worth it. But I appreciate your dedication to getting justice for Evelyn, and I'm sure she would, too."

"There's something I need to say," I said.

"Don't let me stop you."

"One day your conflict with your father is gonna come to a head, and it's not gonna be pretty. I don't like inventing problems that don't exist, but you need to get ahead of him and beat him at his own game."

His eyes narrowed. "You're psychic now?"

Humor might've been a natural defense mechanism, but I wasn't impressed with Liam's response. Not even for a second. Some things weren't funny. I didn't know what I'd do if I lost Liam. Having a relationship that had only just become genuine and public end would've surpassed one of Shakespeare's tragedies.

"I'm serious, Liam."

He ruffled my hair. "I appreciate the concern, but I can defend myself."

"You don't have to put on a façade for me. I'm the last person who would judge you."

"The same goes for you," he said.

I frowned. "Excuse me?"

"It must kill you every day that your father isn't alive. I know that because a part of me died the day Evelyn did."

I looked away from Liam. "I don't wanna talk about that."

"Here's an idea. Let's change the subject."

"Sure," I whispered.

"I've got a question, and it's a good one."

I snickered. "Don't get cocky. You might be hot, but you aren't that hot."

"When did you realize you were in love with me?" Liam asked.

Someone should've pinched me. Not because I was afraid of being honest and vulnerable with Liam; I wasn't. But I'd never expected such a serious remark from him. He might've been making good progress with becoming a decent person, but he still wasn't the most articulate guy.

"Come again?" I asked.

"What? Too early for the L word?"

"I didn't say that. Not gonna deny we've got very intense feelings for each other."

"For me, it was the day I apologized to you," Liam said. "You accepted my remorse even though you had every reason to hate me. That was also the first honest conversation I ever had."

"The evening you wanted to have pizza did it for me. It was the first moment that was more than sex between us."

"Hopefully, there will be lots of pizza in our future," Liam said.

"Here's hoping."

"There's something else I have to say."

"Sure."

"And it's important," he said.

I turned to face Liam. "Go ahead."

"And it's also not out of obligation."

"Just say whatever's on your mind."

"Thank you for taking a chance on me," Liam stammered. "Getting to know you these last few weeks has really been something else."

I was silent for a minute. I couldn't help having butterflies. I didn't need Liam to blatantly tell me how he felt, yet there was something nice about him being so direct. His honesty reaffirmed the realness of our relationship. Being a real couple meant we were supposed to share our feelings with each other.

"Please say something," he said.

"I could say the same about you."

"There's never a dull moment with you."

My hands fell to my sides. "I'll take the compliment."

The patter of outside rain grew louder, then I collapsed onto Liam, head falling on his chest. Thunder roared, but I didn't twitch. Liam and I were where we were supposed to be. Nothing could ruin this moment while his fingers snaked through my hair. Not the weather. Not Evelyn's death. And not Mr. Sinclair. If I had my way, then our time together would last forever. Nobody deserved to be lonely.

I sat in a chair by Natalie's mahogany desk in her bedroom the next day. Outside, rain once again drummed against the ground.

Natalie tapped her hands against her desk. "What do you think?"

I finished reading the last page, then looked up at Natalie. "It's great. But I'm confused why you wanted me here. I'm a photographer, not a writer."

"Doesn't matter. A general artistic overlap exists."

"Sure."

"Was it too blunt?" she asked.

"Not at all." I handed the essay back to her. "You were honest, and that's something most people wouldn't be capable of."

"Really?"

"Yeah. Most people just live with their secrets."

Natalie winked. "Speaking from experience?"

"It's a figure of speech."

"Fair enough."

"I had no idea you liked to write," I said.

Natalie pushed the essay to the side of her desk. "There's something liberating about creative nonfiction."

"I'll take your word for it."

"Hopefully, the essay wins the contest."

I clapped her shoulder. "It will. Have some faith."

"Because it's raw?"

"Yeah." I grabbed pretzels from the glass bowl on the desk.

Natalie remained silent.

"And I'm sorry about your grandfather's stroke—I had no idea it was that bad."

"It was four years ago," she blurted out.

"Doesn't erase the pain."

"Let's change the subject. Would you wanna order some takeout?"

I sneezed, then Natalie handed me a tissue. "I owe you an apology," I said.

Yeah. It was time for me to eat crow. Something had been weighing on my mind ever since I'd become friends with Natalie, Mona, and Gavin again, and I needed to do something about it. When you had the power to change a situation for the positive, it was important to take that step.

She quirked her eyebrows. "For what?"

"I should've been more sensitive about Evelyn outing your crush to the entire school at the beginning of the year."

"Already forgotten about it."

"That couldn't have been fun."

"Don't worry about it," Natalie said. "James came to talk to me the other day."

"Fuck."

Natalie waved her hand. "Relax. This story has a happy ending. He told me he likes me too, and we're gonna hang at some point."

Good for Natalie. I shouldn't have been the only person having fun. Trite as it sounded, she was only young once, and didn't need any regret when she reminisced about her life ten to fifteen years from now.

"What took him so long to man up?" I asked.

"He was embarrassed."

I nodded. "Fair enough."

"How are things with Liam?" She nibbled on another handful of pretzels. "Can I expect wedding bells when you graduate high school?"

"Have your fun. Soon it'll be my turn to make jokes," I said.

"Go ahead—I won't care."

"Anyway, I hope it's okay I couldn't think of any constructive criticism for the essay."

"Enough worrying. I just needed the push to submit it to the contest." Natalie flipped her hair over her shoulders. "Who knows. Maybe you, Liam, Gavin, Mona, James, and I can have a triple date sometime."

Triple date. I couldn't deny the word appealed to me. Another reminder of the normal life I could have instead of contemplating whether my relationship with Liam would implode because of his father—he still didn't know we were dating—or worrying about Evelyn's death.

"What are you thinking about?" Natalie asked.

"What it'd be like to have a normal life." I paused for several seconds. "Do you think that's even possible?"

"If we want it bad enough."

CHAPTER 18

I shuffled into school and approached my locker. I felt warm and hopeful. There was a high chance Liam, and I would cross paths, and he'd give me his usual good morning kiss.

My locker clinked after putting in my combination, but my heart skipped several beats when a folded piece of paper fell from the top locker shelf and onto the ground. I'd watched enough TV shows and movies to know receiving a note in my locker probably wasn't good.

Deep breaths. I couldn't win the game unless I knew what the rules were. So, I unfolded the note: I KNOW YOU KNOW WHO MURDERED EVELYN, AND YOU BETTER DO THE RIGHT THING AND TELL THE POLICE.

Doing a 180 to check my surroundings only made more sweat flop down my face—I was the only person currently in the hallway. I had no fucking clue who might've sent me this cryptic note.

My friends couldn't have written it—I would've recognized their handwriting. They also didn't have a motive for caring about Evelyn's death. Any fleeting sympathy they felt for my grief was because I'd pressured them into that opinion. Liam couldn't have sent me the note, either. I hadn't argued with him after "we" decided not to do anything about how his father had probably killed Evelyn. And Jordon and Evan couldn't have sent it because I hadn't discussed Evelyn's death with them, and they hadn't eavesdropped on any of my conversations about my amateur sleuthing.

My teeth dug into my lip, almost drawing blood. There was something creepy about sending me a note. A text from a blocked number would've been a concrete fact to hold onto, but anyone could've written a note.

I inhaled several long, deep breaths. Maybe I needed a different perspective. The person hadn't threatened me. They just somehow knew the truth about Evelyn's murder. That at least made the situation a little less worrying. So, maybe, just maybe, I had time before my life might implode.

Footsteps echoed and Liam was suddenly there, giving me a quick peck on the lips before picking up the note on the ground.

My throat tightened more with each passing second while Liam twirled it around. He couldn't read it. He just couldn't. Having our relationship in a good place meant not having stupid shit like this ruining our dynamic.

Liam grinned. "Someone write you a love letter?"

"Couldn't be further from the truth." I snatched the note from Liam, then stuffed it into my backpack.

"If you wanna play rough, just ask."

No offense to Liam, but this wasn't the time for flirty banter. Not when my brain was in a whirlwind trying to comprehend someone knowing my "secret." Shit. So much for thinking Liam being closeted from his dad was my biggest problem. I hoped to God there wasn't a way for the universe to prove me wrong even more.

"This isn't funny," I snapped, cheeks becoming warm.

He raised his palms at me. "Just trying to make a joke."

I sighed. "Sorry. I know you mean well—I just failed an English essay yesterday."

Lying to my boyfriend didn't make me a bad person. In this conversation, deception made me practical. Sometimes fibbing was the kindest thing someone could do. Like when you hated a friend's haircut. No harm in saying you liked the new look.

His jaw was almost on the floor. "As in you got an F?"

"Yeah," I mumbled.

"But English is one of your best subjects."

I snickered. "I've lost my touch."

Liam drew me against his body. "I hope that's not true. I'd hate to think what that means for us."

As soon as he touched me, I stopped feeling like a volcano about to erupt. PDA might not have been the first thing on my priority list, but I still vividly remembered the time when Liam wouldn't even chat with me in public.

Gavin gave us a look while darting by. "You two need to get a room."

I stepped back from Liam, almost falling into my locker. "I've been having an off couple of months."

"Because of Evelyn's death?" Liam asked.

"Yes."

"I don't want you to think about that bullshit anymore, man." Liam tickled my nose. "You don't deserve to have my father ruin you."

It was good to know Liam hadn't completely shed his old image, because I didn't know what I would've done if he stopped swearing. Bad language was the kind of not-technically-dangerous edge Liam needed.

"Fine." I grabbed my books and closed my locker. "But I'm still worried about you. You're all alone in that house."

"I spend the night at your house as much as possible."

"That's not my point," I said.

"Okay..."

I stepped closer to Liam, but the words escaped me. I wouldn't say the thought that had popped into my head if my life depended on it. I just couldn't. Not even I was that morbid. Liam also didn't deserve to have his morning ruined.

Liam put his hands on his hips. "Were you gonna say something?"

"Doesn't matter now."

"If something is on your mind, then you need to tell me. Our relationship won't survive unless we have honest communication."

I feigned a smile. "I'm good."

"Whatever."

"How's football going?" I asked.

"Good. But I'm more concerned about you," Liam said. "Positive there's not more than a bad grade going on?"

Crap. Liam was the one person who wouldn't fall for my bullshit.

"I'm good," I said.

Several students flocked down the hallway.

"If you say so," Liam said.

I pouted. "Do you think I'm lying?'

"No. I'm going to trust you until you give me a reason not to," Liam said. "You're not my father—you'd never hurt me for real."

I sat in front of the high school's front entrance several hours later for lunch.

Choosing not to eat with my boyfriend might not have been the nicest thing to do, but I couldn't help myself. Not when I had something more important to focus on.

"The fuck you doing out here?" someone asked.

I lifted my gaze from the various photos on my table. Liam stood in front of me, carrying a lunch tray.

"Nothing," I said.

"I'm not an idiot." He placed his lunch tray on the table, then sat next to me while I shoved my photos into a manila folder. "So please don't insult my intelligence. I want to know about your life."

"Never said you were an idiot."

"Didn't have to."

My brow furrowed. "Still upset about this morning? I thought you said you were gonna believe me until I gave you a reason to doubt me."

"Yeah, I meant what I said."

"Then what's the problem?" I asked.

"I wanna know what's in the folder." Liam took a bite of his sandwich, then took a swig of his chocolate milk.

"Nothing important."

"It can't be worse than anything I've done before."

I squirmed in my seat. I'd wanted Liam to show a different side to me when we started sleeping together, and now I had to do the same thing. But heart palpations weren't necessary. I had to share bits of myself if I wanted to date Liam. I only needed a few seconds to realize that there was such a thing as too much mystery. If Liam didn't have any details about me, then he'd start filling them in himself. And I couldn't have that. Nothing good would arise from it. The extreme side of always making assumptions was paranoia gone amuck. And that wouldn't have been a good look on Liam. Not even for a second.

"Have it your way." I pushed the folder toward Liam. "I'm trying to decide which photos to submit to the Greenwood Guild of Artists show this Saturday night. I can pick up to four photos."

"Was that so hard to say?" Liam put his sandwich back on his tray, then started flipping through the photos. "Damn."

"What's the problem?" I asked.

"You have a lot of photos. Although I'm curious why none of them are of me."

"I didn't need a muse," I said.

Liam kept his eyes on the photos. "Ouch. Maybe I should be offended."

"I was kidding."

"I know. But fuck. You've gotta learn to lighten up." He closed the folder. "Not trying to sound morbid, but you're too young to die of a heart attack."

"Fair enough."

Liam exchanged a look with me. "Do you wanna know my honest opinion?"

"Sure. Go for it."

"You should pick the four photos of yourself."

"And why is that?" I asked.

"I know some things and can guess some others," he said.

I let out a breath. "Okay. Be honest. I promise not to be offended."

"Did you take the four self-portraits within a couple of months of your father's death?"

Wow. Maybe Liam had a future as a fortune teller. There was no way he could've known that, but he did.

"How did you know?" I asked.

"The pain in your eyes."

"Damn."

Liam squeezed my shoulder. "Relax. I meant that in a good way. Your vulnerability is enough to make anyone intoxicated by you."

A nearby squirrel slinked across the grass, then darted up a tree. I must've been having an off week. Liam's comment was almost the same thing I'd said to Natalie about her essay, so I shouldn't have taken the comment to heart so much. Yet here I was, feeling like someone had ripped me open and displayed my insides.

"What time is the show?" Liam asked.

"You don't have to go."

"Don't be ridiculous—I wouldn't miss it for the world."

My gaze shifted to the table counter. "What if someone connected to your dad sees us together and realizes we're a couple?"

"Fuck them."

Color me impressed. Liam had turned into the person I always knew he was capable of becoming—I didn't know if I could've been so bold if the situation reversed itself and I was in Liam's position. I wouldn't have wanted to deal with a violent, alcoholic, homophobic father. Not even if the interaction could've brought my father back to life.

"Excuse me?" I asked.

"I'm serious," Liam said. "My father has stolen a lot of things from me over the years, but I'm not gonna let him take my happiness."

"The show starts at 7:00 P.M., but we should probably get there at 6:45."

"Perfect."

"You don't have a game?" I asked.

"I'd skip if I did. You're more important than football."

"Don't say that—I'd never want you throw away your future because of me."

"Football won't be in my life forever," Liam said.

The chattering of numerous voices vibrated throughout the gallery Saturday evening. I stood in a corner by myself, nestled on the outskirts of the throng.

Liam approached me, handing over a glass of wine. "Here."

"Thanks."

"I remembered you said you hated red wine."

"Yup," I said.

"I don't wanna get your hopes up, but I saw a few people standing by your photos. Maybe you'll make a sale."

"That'd be nice." I sipped my white wine, not even bothering to savor the taste. It wasn't like I was drinking champagne.

"It was shitty of Mona, Natalie, and Gavin not to come," Liam said.

"They had plans."

"Whatever."

"And my mother is out of town again—not that she would care. She's never once told me she was proud of me."

He patted my back. "Well, I'm proud of you."

"Thanks."

Something caught my attention from the corner of my eye, then I shuddered. A person in a black hoodie stood outside of a nearby window, looking me in the face. It was too dark to tell the identity of the person. Not that it mattered—that wasn't the most important issue. What was important was the question that popped into my head as I stared back at them: whether they were the same person who'd left the note in my locker a couple of days ago.

CHAPTER 19

On Tuesday before lunch, another note fell out of my locker.

I picked up the paper, then unfolded it: YOU SHOULD BE ASHAMED OF YOURSELF. YOU'VE GOT THE POWER TO UNMASK EVELYN'S MURDERER, BUT YOU'D RATHER BE A COWARD. SHAME ON YOU.

My breathing became more belabored with each passing second. One note was bad enough. But I couldn't forget about the person standing outside the art gallery the night of the show. A second note was almost the final push to check myself into a mental institution. These were three incidents I couldn't ignore. Didn't even matter that the person hadn't threatened me. They still knew something about me. And I would've been pissed off if the person was wrong, but they weren't. I *was* being a coward by withholding the information I had about Evelyn's death.

Evan and Jordon approached me.

"Hi, man," Evan said.

I crumpled the note. "Hi."

"Something wrong?" Jordon asked.

"No, I'm fine," I said.

Evan coughed. "Liam didn't seem to think so."

"He talked about me behind my back?" I demanded.

Evan sucked on his teeth. "Only out of concern."

"What was the plan?" I stomped my feet against the ground. "Have you two give me some sort of misguided intervention?"

"We care," Evan said.

"I never said you didn't care." I paused for a beat. "What made Liam think I'd be honest with you two? Not like we're best friends."

"Because we know about last May," Jordon said.

Damn. Whether I liked the truth or not, everything in my life returned to Evelyn's Spring Fling party or the Monday morning after the event. And that was just great. I *so* wanted to be tied to the same one or two events for the rest of my life.

I forced in a breath. "Oh."

Evan glanced at the note in my right hand, then made eye contact. "Someone giving you a hard time?"

"Not exactly," I said.

Jordon's eyebrows shot up. "It's more than failing an English essay, isn't it?"

"Liam told you about that?" I asked.

Jordon nodded at me. "Yep."

"Liam should've just kept his damn mouth shut!" I almost yelled. "He has no clue what's going on."

"You better start talking," Evan said.

I sneered. "I don't have to do anything I don't wanna do."

"True. But the anger isn't gonna go to a good place," Jordon pointed out.

No shit. I didn't need Jordon to tell me that. I hadn't forgotten what Liam's homophobic anger had made him do to me.

"Don't psychoanalyze me!" I snapped.

"We're trying to be decent people," Evan said.

"Nobody asked you to save me. Don't you have your own lives to worry about?"

Jordon pressed his palms together. "Promise not to judge."

"That's what people say right before making a judgment," I said.

"We aren't Liam's dad." Evan looked defensive.

Liam scurried over to us, but I stepped back when he was about to kiss me.

"What gives?" Liam asked.

"You had no right asking Tweedle Dee and Tweedle Dumb to talk with me," I said. "You should've respected my privacy."

Liam's face drooped. "I was concerned about you."

Funny he should say that. If that was really true, then he should've showed his worry in a different way. I had shared something personal—my photography—despite the risk of doing so. Sex and nudity weren't the only scenarios that made me feel like I had everything to lose. I'd had no way of knowing how Liam would react my photos. More specifically, the photographs showing my grief.

I hissed at Liam. "You wanna know why I've been on edge? It's because someone knows we know your father killed Evelyn and aren't doing anything about it."

"The fuck you talking about?" Liam asked.

I shoved the note at Liam. "See for yourself."

Liam took the note from me, studying it for a good minute or two before handing the paper to Evan and Jordon.

"It's the second one I got," I said through gritted teeth. "And this person might be stalking me. Someone was standing outside the gallery the night of my show."

"Why didn't you say anything?" Liam's eyebrows drew down.

"You're the one who doesn't care about your dad killing Evelyn," I said.

Liam stared. A bead of sweat formed on his forehead and he wiped it away. "That's not true and you know it. You don't understand how complicated the situation is."

Evan tugged at his Letterman jacket pockets. "The person would be more direct if they wanted to hurt you."

"Evan is right," Jordon said.

Liam put his arms around my neck, but I refused to make eye contact. I couldn't tell Liam how to live his life, yet a small part of me couldn't help being pissed. Having closure about Evelyn's death—like Liam's father being held accountable—was important. Deep breaths, though. I couldn't let my difference of opinion fester. Mr. Sinclair was Liam's father, not mine.

The bell rang.

"Will you do something for me?" Liam asked.

"Doubtful!" I laughed.

"Please," he whispered.

Several students darted by.

I folded my arms. "What?"

He remained silent for a second. "Tell me right away if you have a problem next time—I can't help you if I don't know what's wrong."

I heaved out a sigh. Liam had a point, even if I didn't want to admit the truth. Staying silent was one of the dumbest things somebody trying to have a healthy relationship could do. Liam wasn't only my boyfriend. He was also a lifeline. And no matter how much rage or fear might've flared through my body, I couldn't be my own worst enemy.

"Fine," I said.

He stroked my chin. "Good. Because I couldn't take you being mad at me much longer."

"Maybe you need to relax," I said.

Liam wiggled his eyebrows. "Maybe."

Evan rolled his eyes. "Gavin was right the other day. You two really need to get a room."

Jordon jabbed Evan's shoulder. "I don't remember you caring about getting a room when you were drooling over Penelope last year."

"Whatever," Evan said.

"Why don't I walk you to first period?" Liam asked me.

I let out a small laugh. "We're in the same class."

Liam playfully elbowed me. "All the more reason for me to walk you."

Liam took my hand and we strutted down the hallway. My breathing slowed—almost as if I'd found a well of water after journeying through a desert. Liam and I had had our first major "fight," yet we'd survived. Maybe, just maybe, I needed to have more faith in our relationship. Bickering wasn't always toxic and violent. Suppressing my feelings would've only made the situation messier.

Moonlight glinted against the high school parking lot Friday night while I stood by my Mercedes after the football game.

Liam cut through the crowd of people, making his way over to me.

"I'm so proud of you for scoring the winning touchdown," I said.

"Thanks," Liam said.

I stayed silent while his cheeks turned a bright shade of scarlet.

"Still wanna go to the party?" he asked.

"Yup. Mom doesn't get back 'til Monday."

Liam adjusted his Letterman jacket's collar. "Coming to the game was nice of you. I know sports isn't your thing."

"Not a big deal. Not like I had anything better to do."

"Dad should be ashamed of himself for not coming," Liam blurted.

Poor Liam. I didn't know what I would've done if I were him. He should've been able to escape his father for one fleeting moment. Liam didn't deserve to have him controlling every second of his life.

I rocked my hands back and forth. "Maybe it's a blessing in disguise."

"Probably," Liam said.

Thank goodness he agreed with me. I hadn't considered my response at first but being more considerate might've been best. I shouldn't have told Liam — an abuse victim — how to feel.

"We kind of said the 'L' word to each other and had our first real argument, but we're still standing," I said.

Liam gave me a look. "Why wouldn't I tell you I love you? It's the truth."

"I know, I know."

"You're the one good thing in my life."

Liam didn't wait for me to respond. Instead, he drew me against his body and kissed me. Even though voices still reverberated through the parking lot. Almost as if he were saying, 'the rest of the world be damned.' For the moment, our relationship was the only thing that mattered. And that was okay. We were only seventeen, and that was the way life was supposed to be.

I pushed a lock of my hair out of the way while Liam and I were in bed sometime later. Music from the next room pulsed through the wall.

"We're gonna be in so much trouble," I said.

"For what?" Liam asked.

"We went to the football team's victory party just to sneak away to have sex."

"They'd be happy for me."

I exploded into laughter. "If you say so."

"But maybe I should make an appearance," he said. "Can I get you anything to drink? I'm gonna get myself a Rum and Diet Coke."

"I'll have what you're having."

"Perfect." Liam grabbed his clothes from the middle of the bed. He slid into his them and looked back at me. "Shit. Will you be fine by yourself?"

"Yeah. I haven't gotten another note."

"Cool." He kissed me before hopping out of the bed and walking towards the door. He was gone in a matter of seconds.

I placed my head on the pillow behind me.

I couldn't help being grateful, though that might've been another trite sentiment. I deserved wins, and I was getting them. If someone had asked me last year if I'd be dating Liam Sinclair or attending the football team's victory party, I would've told the person they were crazy.

But no. Life was stranger than people realized.

I woke up sometime later—still in the same bed—to the sound of the door creaking. A person in a black hoodie and matching black pants entered the bedroom. I cocked my head around. Liam was nowhere to be seen.

The person began scurrying towards me.

My stomach might as well have been ripped out of my body and tied around my throat. I'd have to pass the person to get out of the bedroom, so there was no point in jumping from the bed.

My eyes darted to the lamp on the table to the right of me. The person was only a few feet away, so I unplugged the lamp and gripped it with both hands.

The person hovered over me.

Damn. If they were about to terrorize me, then I deserved to know who my tormentor was. It was only fair.

The person yanked their hood down. It was Violet Judd—Evelyn's best friend and the daughter of the older man Evelyn had had an affair with.

"What the hell?" I blinked.

Violet giggled. "Hello, Connor. Great to see you."

CHAPTER 20

"Are you gonna kill me?" I asked.

Violet scoffed. "Don't be ridiculous. I just wanna chat."

My grip on the lamp tightened. "You were the one who sent me the two notes and stood outside the gallery the night I debuted?"

Violet nodded. "Yes."

"What game are you playing?" I asked.

Violet gave me a dirty look. "You can drop the lamp. If I wanted to kill you, then you'd be dead. I'm not a liar—unlike some people."

The goosebumps clinging to my arms, legs, and back didn't disappear. I didn't want to even consider being murdered. Losing Evelyn had been bad enough. Life should've been getting less morbid, not more.

"You've got some explaining to do," I said.

Violet winked. "The footsteps you heard that day in the hallway? When you told your friends everything about Evelyn? That was me."

The lamp fell onto the bed, then I stroked my chin. So, the footsteps hadn't been a random passerby. I should've inferred the universe had other plans for me. Violet was just the complication I needed right now.

"You didn't answer my question," I spat. "Who cares if I don't go to the police? Why not contact them yourself?"

Violet giggled, making my back hairs rise. "Really that dense?"

"Don't insult me," I said. "I could scream at any moment."

"But you won't," Violet said. "You would've tried to leave the room if you thought I wanted to murder you."

"You don't hate Evelyn?" I asked.

Violet let out a long breath. "Evelyn isn't the first time my father's cheated. Besides, she didn't deserve to die. I'm sure we can agree on that."

A kinder person would've empathized with Violet about her father's indiscretions, but I didn't. She got shits and giggles from psychologically terrorizing me. Forgiveness was sometimes overrated—my feelings were what mattered in this situation, not Violet's.

"The situation is more complicated than you think," I said.

Violet rolled her eyes. "Sounds like an excuse."

I whipped my head back and forth. "Liam's father is an abusive, homophobic drunk, but apparently being a selfish bitch is the only thing that matters to you."

"Watch yourself."

"I'm not afraid of you," I said.

Violet sniggered. "Might wanna take some acting classes."

I rubbed my temple. "Liam has nothing tying his father to the murder other than the cigarette butt he discovered by Evelyn's body."

Violet's blank expression remained plastered on her face. "Doesn't matter."

I snarled. "Wanna know what I think? You're looking for an outlet for your anger about your dad cheating, and Evelyn's death is the most expedient way of doing that."

"Maybe. Maybe not."

The door opened and Liam walked in. He was carrying a cup in each hand.

Thank goodness Liam had arrived, because I couldn't take one more minute of chatting with Violet. We were wasting time with our conversation. She'd never understand my point of view.

"What the hell is going on?" Liam asked.

My eyes moved toward him. "Violet knows everything. She overheard me telling Mona, Natalie, and Gavin about our theory."

Liam gave me a funny look. "The fuck you talking about?"

"I'm not joking," I said.

Liam placed the drinks on the table by the door, then raced over to the bed. He stood in front of me, blocking Violet from where I sat.

Violet played with her pigtails. "If Liam was so concerned about his father, then he wouldn't have gone public with your relationship."

"Our relationship is none of your fucking business, bitch," Liam said.

"Careful. I'm nice, but not that nice," Violet said.

"Was that a threat?" I asked.

Violet gave me a hyena-like smile. "Just stating a fact."

"You've got some fucking nerve accosting Connor." Liam put a hand on my shoulder. "You aren't the morality police."

Violet expelled a sharp giggle. "You should want justice for your sister."

Wow. Apparently, Violet was even pushier than I was. She shouldn't have been telling Liam how to feel about his sister's death. It was the most condescending thing she could've done. If the situation reversed itself, and someone told Violet how she needed to behave, she would've lost her shit.

"You haven't met my father," Liam said.

"No, I haven't," Violet agreed.

"She's also the person who sent me the two letters and stalked me the night of my show at the gallery," I cut over her.

"No offense, but I figured that part out for myself," Liam said.

"I'm serious," Violet said. "You two better fucking go to the police or *I'm* going to go to the police."

I glared at Violet. "Why don't you go to the police if this such big deal to you?"

Violet nibbled on the inside of her lip. "I didn't wanna make my life more complicated. Evelyn was also both your best friend and Liam's sister…"

"You don't scare us," Liam said.

Violet ran her fingers through her hair. "I should."

Music continued to blare from the next room. It was muffled by the walls around us, enhancing my sensation of being trapped and separated from the rest of the house.

"Enough!" I exclaimed. "You're gonna let this situation go, Violet."

Violet's smile widened. "Go ahead. Convince me."

"Liam and I still have Evelyn's diary and the bartender at the restaurant your father and Evelyn went to will corroborate how they were involved," I said, chin raised.

If the situation wasn't so serious, I could've chuckled. Violet had accused me of being dumb, so she should've been smart enough herself to realize what my intentions were. It wasn't like I'd asked her to solve a Calculus problem.

"What's your point?" Violet asked.

"If you continue pushing us to go to the police, then Liam and I will leak everything about the affair!" I barked.

Violet's pupils dilated. "You wouldn't."

"Evelyn is already dead," I said flatly. "This would hurt your father more than it would ruin Evelyn's reputation—everyone already knew Evelyn could be a bitch sometimes. No offense, Liam."

"None taken," Liam said.

Violet kicked her feet against the ground. "Son of a bitch!"

"Do we have an agreement?" I asked, staring Violet down.

Violet grunted. "Yes."

I stepped closer to Violet. "Then leave. I don't ever wanna see your face again."

Violet licked her lips at Liam. "I'd be careful if I were you. It's always the nice ones you have to watch out for. At least Evelyn never pretended to be a good person."

"Your point being?" Liam asked.

Her eyes beamed. "Fucking Connor will only get you so far. You're playing with fire and are gonna get burned one day."

Liam cackled. "I'll take my chances."

I was grateful Liam hadn't stopped me from blackmailing Violet. If he wanted to be my boyfriend and have a real relationship, then he needed to accept every part of me. Including the side of me that thought morality was sometimes overrated. I'd done what needed to be done and wouldn't stare at my bedroom ceiling longer than normal pondering my actions when I went to bed after the party.

I shouted at Violet. "Leave!"

Violet left the bedroom, slamming the door behind her.

I grabbed my clothes from under the pillow behind me and changed into them before jumping out of bed.

I gave Liam a weak smile. "Thanks for not judging me about how I handled Violet. Some people might not approve."

"Being your boyfriend means not thanking me for anything."

Boyfriend. The word's appeal never got old. Like it or not, Liam was the one person aside from my mom who'd always see the best in me. And I needed that more than anything. Mom might not have cared about me being sexually active, but she would probably lecture me about not blackmailing people. I still hadn't forgotten the time she'd chastised me about cheating on an extra credit assignment. She'd lectured me about the cheating for a good month. In fact, I'd originally thought that she'd never stop rambling about the incident.

"I'm sorry, but I wanna go home," I said.

"That's fine."

"I can drop you off around the block from your house."

"Won't be necessary. He doesn't expect me home tonight," Liam said.

He. A single word shouldn't have had so much impact, but it did. Liam couldn't even refer to Mr. Sinclair as "dad" or "father," and my heart once again broke again for him. I couldn't even fathom being in that position. At least Evelyn being alive had provided a buffer between him and his father.

"Okay. Cool," I said.

"But I should drive."

"I only had one drink, and that was when we first got here."

"That's not what I'm worried about, silly."

"Oh…"

Liam's face softened. "Anyone would be stressed if they were in your position."

"I know, I know."

"Although I should apologize."

"For what?" I asked.

"I shouldn't have left you alone for so long. Evan and Jordon just started rambling and wouldn't shut up."

"Don't worry about it."

Liam and I stood next to each other as afternoon sunlight spilled into my kitchen.

"Color me shocked," Liam said. "Never would've pictured us making brownies."

"It's something fun and different."

"Because of yesterday?"

"Let's not talk about Violet." I grabbed an egg from the carton, cracked it into a metal mixing bowl, then did the same thing again.

"If it makes you feel better, I don't think she was lying. She has nothing to gain from hurting you."

"If you say so." I grabbed a whisk from the drawer, then stirred the mix. "You never mentioned what Jordon and Evan were babbling about."

"Not important."

A cynical person might've thought Liam was hiding something. But not me. I had enough problems without considering that Liam might be keeping secrets. I also had no reason to doubt him and wanted him to give me the same courtesy.

"Fair enough," I said. "Anyway, I've been doing all the work while you're standing here doing nothing."

"Don't be overdramatic."

"I'm serious."

"I can't help it if I'm intoxicated by my hot boyfriend."

"I bet you'd use that line on anyone." I put the whisk in the sink after I finished stirring. After that, I poured the brownies into the tray, which I'd already coated with a non-stick spray. "No offense or anything."

"Actually, I wouldn't use that line on just anyone. You're my first serious relationship," he said. "You should know that…"

"I was teasing."

"I know."

The oven beeped. I put the tray inside, then snatched the metal mixing bowl and a nearby spoon from the counter and started eating the remaining brownie batter. I waved the bowl at Liam. "Want some?"

"Gross."

"Excuse me?"

He wrinkled his nose. "Don't you worry about getting sick from the raw egg?"

"Live on the wild side."

"No thanks. I'll leave that to you."

"Whatever." I finished off the batter and dumped the metal bowl in the sink.

Liam wet his right index finger, then wiped some chocolate off my mouth before sucking on his finger.

"What about the raw egg?" I demanded.

"No harm in one taste."

Liam undid the top button of his flannel shirt, then fanned himself with the fabric. "Maybe baking when the temperature's back in the seventies wasn't the smartest idea."

"Whatever."

"I can't help it if I'm sensitive to the heat."

"Sound just like my grandmother," I said. "She can tolerate the cold but is about ready to die if she doesn't have air conditioning in the summer."

"My kind of person."

"Anyway, would you like to go out for lunch after this?"

Liam nodded. "Sure. Have something in mind?

CHAPTER 21

Liam and I lay stretched across my bed hours after baking brownies. He scooted closer. "What are you thinking about?"

"Some thoughts are better left unsaid."

Liam gave me wry smile. "Really gonna try that bullshit with me? Weren't we supposed to be past the games by now?"

"Don't make me lie to you."

"I promise not to get mad. Even if you think I'm ugly."

Ouch. Maybe Liam's self-esteem was still lower than I realized. I knew *I* would've felt like less than shit in Liam's position. No amount of empathy could let me know what it was to actually live Liam's experiences with his father.

I made an almost pig-like snort. "I'd never say something that dumb."

Liam stroked my hair. "Doesn't matter. I wouldn't judge you if you did. Consider this your get-out-of-jail-free card."

"How can you live with your father getting away with everything?" I asked.

"We already had this discussion."

"You said I could say anything."

He bit his lip. "You're right. I'm sorry."

"Not trying to upset you. Just refuse to believe that English class is telling the truth."

"The fuck you talking about?"

"About life being unfair," I said. "If crime didn't pay, then nobody would do it. Innocent people are blamed for things while guilty people get away with abominations all the time."

"Someone's using some big words," Liam said.

My eyes almost rolled out of their sockets. In a perfect world, Liam wouldn't have used humor as a coping mechanism.

"This isn't a joke, Liam." I paused for a long time before coughing, clearing the nervousness from my throat. "I need you to be honest with me like I was with you."

"Okay."

"Do you have any doubts about your father's guilt?" I asked. "It's okay if you do, but you've gotta tell me. I can't read your mind."

"Nope."

"Then what's the problem?"

Liam looked away. "He's a monster."

"What's the plan for the rest of your life?" I asked. "Cut him out after you finish college?"

"I have nobody, Connor."

"You've got me," I said, raising my voice.

"That's not what I meant, and you know it. I'm just in a different position than you. Having a shitty home life is the only thing I've ever known."

Someone could've kicked me in the balls, and it would've hurt less.

It wasn't my fault Mom had treated me better than Liam's father did him. It wasn't like I reminded Liam of the difference in our situations on a regular basis.

"Sorry I asked," I said.

"It's okay," he whispered. "I said you could be honest and I'm not gonna change my mind because I don't like what you said."

"If you don't wanna cause trouble, then I respect your decision," I said.

"Thank you."

"You don't have to stay the night if you don't want to."

Liam batted his eyes. "Kicking me out?"

If I didn't know better, I was experiencing some déjà vu. Sleeping together didn't mean we had to wake up to each other almost every morning. Especially when I wasn't sure how I should feel about our difference of opinion on his father's involvement in Evelyn's murder.

"Just being honest," I said.

He squeezed my hand. "I'm not gonna run because of some minor disagreement."

Good to know he wasn't a complete coward, because that was the word I would've used to describe Liam's behavior towards his father. He'd never have emotional stability unless he removed his father from his life. In a way, Mr. Sinclair resembled a cancer that needed to be eradicated. Better Mr. Sinclair die than Liam.

I couldn't swallow the lump in my throat. "Good to know."

"We aren't always gonna agree on everything, and that's okay." Liam sat up in bed. "The point is we just gotta respect each other."

"If you say so."

"My turn to ask a question," he said. "I need to know that you'll be able to let this go."

"Absolutely," I lied.

Mona, Gavin, Liam, and I sat at a table in the back of the Greenwood Grille several evenings later, sipping flavored iced teas.

Mona opened her purse, then coated her lips with a fresh layer of bright purple lipstick. "Nice we're doing this. Feels like I haven't seen you in ages, Connor."

"Don't be so theatrical." I sipped my iced tea, letting the peach flavor linger on my tongue before swallowing the liquid.

Mona leaned forward after shoving her lipstick back in her purse. "I didn't even get to talk to you at the football team's victory party."

"Chill out," Gavin said.

I nodded. "What Gavin said."

Liam's gaze remained on the menu while the overhead lights became dim.

"Something wrong?" I whispered into Liam's right ear.

"Trying to figure out what to order," Liam said.

Thank goodness that was all. I didn't know what I would've done if he was pissed about our conversation the other day. Especially because nothing good could come from discussing the issue with him. The problem only had one clear solution. Somehow, I would survive it.

"So many good choices," Gavin said.

Mona wrapped a strand of hair around her finger. "I always order the salad when Gavin and I come here."

Gavin shook his head. "Yeah, I know."

"Problem with me getting a salad?" Mona asked.

Gavin gave Mona a playful look. "You deserve something exciting."

"Don't be silly." Mona straightened. "But enough serious talk. I propose a toast."

I almost choked on my iced tea "To what?"

"Finally having a double date," Mona said.

"Good a reason as any," Liam said.

We clinked our glasses together before chugging more of our beverages.

All my interactions with Liam—from when we'd first met at the Spring Fling party to our double date tonight—played through my mind like a movie montage. I would never have guessed the guy I'd fooled around with at a random party last year would someday be comfortable enough to hang with me and my friends in public, let alone become my boyfriend.

I rang Liam's doorbell the following evening while stars illuminated the night sky and an owl sitting on a nearby tree hooted.

Liam had an away football game, so I wouldn't worry about him ruining my plans. Really, it was better this way. Sometimes ignorance helped people. Liam could never know about what I was gonna do.

I pressed the doorbell several more times.

The door opened, revealing Mr. Sinclair.

"What the fuck are you doing here, faggot?" Mr. Sinclair asked, slurring his words.

I raised my gun at him. "Surprise, bitch."

"What the fuck did you just say?" he asked.

"Yeah, I called you a bitch," I said. "But that's not your biggest problem."

"Oh?"

My fingers remained on the trigger. "If you don't let me in your house, then I'm gonna blow your brains out."

CHAPTER 22

I stood in my kitchen hours after my chat with Mr. Sinclair, right hand still on Mom's gun. One quick glance down created a mountain of tension in my shoulders—blood coated my hands.

Sweat dripped down my back as my encounter with Mr. Sinclair etched itself into my mind over and over. The old me wouldn't have had the balls to confront a volatile drunk. But I hadn't had a choice. And it hadn't only been about getting justice for Evelyn. Liam and I wouldn't have a real future unless Mr. Sinclair was banished from our lives.

The doorbell rang and my breathing grew heavier. The person would leave. If I wanted something badly enough, then it would come true. That was an unwritten law of the universe. My breaths would slow down eventually and I'd wash the blood off my hands. I had to. If I was serious about removing Mr. Sinclair from my life, then I couldn't leave any traces of what I'd done behind.

The doorbell beeped several more times.

Damn. If the person was being this persistent, then the issue must've been important.

I'd wash the blood off my hands first, though. If I didn't, then I deserved to be caught. Even I couldn't be that stupid.

I put the gun on the kitchen counter, then yanked the faucet. Water flowed from the sink and I scrubbed the blood off my hands. I turned the sink off a moment later, then dried my hands with a nearby towel.

Cleaning my hands was one thing, but I wouldn't abandon Mom's gun. Not yet. It was possible I would need it for protection. No telling who was waiting for me on the front porch.

The doorbell buzzed again, and I marched out of the kitchen after grabbing the gun. I opened the door, discovering Gavin.

"What's up?" I asked.

"Liam has sent you half a dozen calls and texts and hasn't heard back from you about the party after tonight's game," Gavin said. "Everything okay?"

I whipped my iPhone out of my jacket pocket with my free hand, then pressed the Home button. I had six unread text messages and six voicemails, all from Liam. Wow. So much for hoping he wouldn't complicate tonight.

Gavin's focus shifted to my gun—which had slipped into his line of sight as my attention moved to my phone—and his eyes widened before he made eye contact again. "What the fuck is going on, man?"

I shoved the gun behind my leg. "It's complicated."

"That's not an answer."

I tousled my hair up, averting my gaze. "I can't do this right now."

Gavin folded his arms. "Are you in trouble?"

"I don't have time for this."

"Would you rather I call your mother?" he asked.

"You're bluffing."

"I'm not. She gave me her cellphone number in case of emergencies."

I scowled. "Fucking fantastic."

"Why don't you let me inside? Maybe you'll feel more comfortable talking in your own home where nobody can see us."

"Good idea." I threw a glance behind me.

Gavin entered my home, and I locked the door behind him.

"If I'm your best friend, then I deserve honesty," Gavin said.

My body burned with guilt, which was the last thing I needed right now. It wasn't as if my jaw was still shaking.

"It involves Mr. Sinclair," I said.

Gavin's eyebrows slid up. "Did you kill him?"

"Not exactly."

"What the hell does that mean?"

"It's complicated."

"I'm not leaving until you tell me the truth. Even if it means staying here all night, because don't think I won't do that."

I let out the loudest sigh of my life. I couldn't believe it. My plan was blowing up in my face now that Gavin was gonna make me discuss what had happened, and nothing I did would change his mind. The stern look hadn't disappeared from Gavin's face. I was fucked. I just hoped Gavin wouldn't judge me—a real friend wouldn't. Even if my encounter with Mr. Sinclair might've been the most violent moment of my life.

I hadn't lowered the gun while Mr. Sinclair and I stood by his front door. "I'm serious, asshole. Are you gonna let me in or what?"

"Make it fast. I don't normally associate with faggots."

"You must be proud of yourself." I trekked into Liam's house, then grabbed my iPhone from my jacket pocket, gun still pointed at Mr. Sinclair with my free hand. I turned my iPhone on, pulled up an app, then pressed record before stuffing my phone back into my jacket pocket.

"I want something from you, and you're gonna give it to me."

"And what's that?" Mr. Sinclair grabbed the bottle of whiskey on the table by the front door and chugged a third of it.

"I know Evelyn's death was a murder, not an accident. You must've overheard her conversation with Liam. The one about how she was pregnant and didn't wanna get an abortion."

Mr. Sinclair sipped more whiskey, then belched. "I'm impressed."

"Is that a confession?"

"Fine," Mr. Sinclair bellowed. "I'll be merciful and grant your dumb faggot ass this one request. Yeah, I hated that Evelyn was involved with an older man and wouldn't get an abortion. Liam is disgrace enough."

My stomach sank. Listening to Liam talk about what a shitty person his father was and hearing these remarks directly from Mr. Sinclair were two different things. No wonder Liam almost hadn't been able to show me the real version of himself. I didn't know what I would've done if I had a parent who kicked me before I got my bearings each day.

"Good to know I was right," I said.

Instead of answering, Mr. Sinclair finished the whiskey on the table and dropped the bottle onto the floor, scattering glass shards across the carpet.

"Sorry," Mr. Sinclair mumbled. "My grip isn't what it used to be."

"Might wanna think about cutting back."

Mr. Sinclair laughed. "You're hilarious."

"Why be honest with me? Because I'm holding a gun?"

"That. And because you can't prove a fucking thing."

"True."

Mr. Sinclair rubbed his hands together. "I have no regrets. I wanted Evelyn dead, and she got what she deserved."

"You're right." I grabbed my iPhone from my pocket, free hand keeping the gun elevated at Mr. Sinclair. I stopped the recording and pushed my iPhone back into my pocket. "I can't prove anything."

"Just fucking go!" Mr. Sinclair exclaimed.

"One more thing," I said.

He raised his brow. "And what's that?"

I rushed towards Mr. Sinclair, then shoved him against the wall. In his drunken state, his reflexes were slowed enough that he didn't resist. I pistol whipped him with the gun, drawing blood.

"That was for Evelyn." I threw Mr. Sinclair onto the ground, then kneeled and punched him in the face several times. "And that's for Liam."

"I'm impressed," Mr. Sinclair whimpered. "Fag fights back."

I stood, then kicked Mr. Sinclair in the balls. "If you ever hurt Liam, I'll fucking kill you."

"You'll pay for this," Mr. Sinclair said.

"Doubtful. With a little luck, you'll choke on your own vomit."

"I can't believe you did that," Gavin said, drawing me out of my digression.

I started crying. "Please don't turn me into the police or tell Liam what I did. I didn't actually try and kill his father."

He gripped my shoulders, then stared me down. "I'm not gonna snitch on you, but you should consider telling Liam the truth. These types of situations usually come back to ruin people. And I'd hate to see anything bad happen to you or your relationship."

"Gavin, please…"

He grimaced. "Promise me one thing. Don't confront Mr. Sinclair again. What if he isn't as drunk next time?"

"Meaning?"

"You got lucky with him not fighting back," Gavin said. "Next time, that might not happen."

Dread lingered in my throat. Gavin was right, whether I told him I agreed with him or not. I'd had no way of knowing how drunk Mr. Sinclair would be before I headed to Liam's house, and I didn't know what I would've done if he'd defended himself.

"Fine," I finally said. "I'll stay away from Mr. Sinclair."

"Good."

CHAPTER 23

I sat in the front passenger seat of Liam's car the following Friday evening while the vehicle barreled down a new stretch of highway. My gaze remained glued to the window, and Liam coughed.

"We need to talk," Liam said.

"Okay."

"I know you've been keeping something from me."

If Liam had connected the dots about my absence that night, then he should've just said so. Unless he wanted to hear the truth from me. It was a possibility.

My shoulders tensed. "Don't be absurd."

"You still haven't explained why you missed my calls and texts after the game last week."

"I was exhausted. I fell asleep from doing schoolwork."

"I don't believe you," Liam said.

"Never gave you a reason to doubt me."

"Secrets are toxic."

I snickered. "Really gonna pull that crap with me? You're were closeted for years. You even beat me up because I talked to you in public the Monday after the Spring Fling."

Liam honked his horn at the car in front of us, which was driving a little too slowly. "I apologized."

"Did someone say something to you?"

My fingers tingled while I looked at Liam, waiting for a response. Hopefully Mr. Sinclair hadn't snitched on me. Liam asking me a question he already knew the answer to would've been messed up. If Liam wanted to say something, he should've just made his comment.

Mr. Sinclair couldn't have told Liam about our altercation, though. Admitting a "faggot" had knocked him on his ass would've been a huge concession. So the truth about that night was still a mystery to Liam. It had to be.

"Like who?" he asked.

"Never mind."

"If you're honest with me, then I promise not to be angry with you. Nothing is too bad to tell me."

I nibbled on the inside of my lip. Honesty might've been best. Not because I owed Liam anything or felt some kind of guilt, but because it was better Liam hear I attacked his father from me than someone else.

"I confronted your dad the night of your football game," I said. "I even recorded his confession on my iPhone."

"You did what?" Liam halted at a red light.

"Not like I went to the police."

"Why not?"

"I don't know what to do with this. It's not immiscible in court in this state." I caught my breath. "Maybe I could use it to force him into turning himself in—you know, threaten to leak the recording to the media."

Liam remained silent, continuing to drive.

"Do you hate me?" I asked.

Liam once again remained silent.

"Say something," I said.

"We agreed to do nothing about my father's involvement in Evelyn's death. Or maybe you were lying to me."

"I meant it when I said it."

"What changed?" Liam asked.

"It's not fair he's getting away with everything."

"Not your call to make."

"Do you wanna break up with me?" I asked.

"You think that little of me?"

"Don't put words in my mouth."

"I'm not gonna ditch you because we're going through a brief rough patch." Liam smacked his car horn again. "Contrary to what people think, I'm a good person."

"Never said you weren't."

"Please tell me you didn't out me to my father."

Liam should've known better than to ask that question. I had nothing to gain by making Liam's life more miserable. I'd also stopped myself from outing him in front of Evan and Jordon that day at lunch, so I had restraint.

"I didn't," I said.

"Then we're good."

"For real?" I asked after blinking several times.

"You were Evelyn's best friend, so I understand where you're coming from."

"Where does your dad think you're going this weekend?" I asked.

"To a friend's house."

"Cool."

Liam shot me an apologetic look. "You know I'd come out to my father if it mattered."

"No explanation necessary."

"I'm guessing you attacked him?" Liam asked. "I might be a lot of things, but I'm not dumb. I saw his bruises."

"I brought my mother's gun with me." I had no problem admitting to that part of the story. It wasn't like Liam's opinion of me could get any worse.

"Fuck." Liam exploded into laughter. "You weren't playing a game."

"Nope."

"You could've gotten hurt."

"Doesn't matter," I said. "Anyway, you never told me where your father thinks you are when you spend the night at my house."

"Hanging with my football buddies."

"There's always emancipation. Or you could become a foster kid," I said.

"The allowance my father gives me wouldn't cover the cost of a lawyer, and you can't really be tone-deaf enough to suggest foster care."

"Sorry," I murmured.

"The important thing is we're gonna enjoy the weekend at my family's cabin."

Liam had a point. His father had done a lot of damage already, and we couldn't let him ruin our getaway, too. This weekend was an opportunity to escape, and Liam and I would've been stupid not to take it. No telling when we'd get another opportunity for a whole weekend to ourselves.

"Fair enough," I said.

Liam and I sat on a couch sometime later, watching a movie on the living room TV at his cabin. He grabbed the remote, then paused the movie.

"Something wrong?" I asked.

"Why are you with me?" Liam asked.

Damn. Not exactly the type of thing I wanted to hear right now. Nothing like a huge existential question a couple of hours before bed. I had no idea what had prompted Liam to ask it. I couldn't help wondering if we were headed for another argument. He might not have been over me meddling by playing amateur detective—I probably wouldn't have been the bigger person if I were in his position. Trust was the foundation of every good relationship, and I wouldn't have dated someone if I constantly needed to wonder when the next time they'd go behind my back would be.

"We've already had this discussion." My hands fell to my lap. "I saw a different side of you the night you had pizza with me instead of just hooking up."

"Not referring to that," Liam said. "What do you actually see in me? You mentioned me punching you again. Been a few times now."

"I was angry."

"It was still on your mind."

"Sorry. I fucked up."

"You really aren't angry about what I did?" Liam asked.

"I wasn't the nicest person either after my father died."

"Find that hard to believe."

"It's the truth." I broke eye contact with Liam. "I could ask the same thing about why you're with me. Desperate for someone to love you or just horny?"

Muffled footsteps sounded outside and suddenly the front door burst open. Someone cackled and Liam and I looked up. Mr. Sinclair stood in front of us.

"What are you doing here?" Liam asked.

Someone might as well have ripped my lungs from my chest. Liam's father couldn't have been a couple of feet from us. Yet he was. No amount of blinking made him any less present.

"I'm the adult, so I'll ask the questions," Mr. Sinclair said.

"I thought you were supervising the gardeners this weekend," Liam stuttered.

"I put a tracker on your car tire a couple of days ago," Mr. Sinclair said.

Liam and I exchanged a stolen glance. Shit. If Mr. Sinclair was tracking Liam's whereabouts, then he might've known Liam had slept over at my house the last couple of nights. I could've been suffocating on dirt. If Liam and I didn't act quickly, then Mr. Sinclair would realize we were dating—if he didn't already know, that was.

"You've got some nerve corrupting my son, faggot," Mr. Sinclair said, slurring his words.

"Did you drive drunk?" Liam asked.

Mr. Sinclair's eyebrows knitted together. "Doesn't matter."

"Nothing is going on," I hastened to say.

Mr. Sinclair cackled louder this time. "And I'm the fucking King of England."

"You can't prove anything," Liam said.

Mr. Sinclair's eyes widened. "You two are obviously dating."

"Two guys can be friends," I protested.

Liam stood. "Fine. You're right."

Mr. Sinclair didn't speak.

Liam squeezed my hand. "Connor is my boyfriend and makes me happy. And there's not a fucking thing you can do about it."

Someone needed to slap me. I must've been having a nightmare. I didn't need a crystal ball to know that this situation could only have one outcome, and it didn't involve sunshine and rainbows.

Mr. Sinclair inhaled sharply, but still didn't speak.

"Wanna know something else?" Liam asked. "I was fucking Connor that day my bedroom door was locked. The day I said I was with a girl."

Mr. Sinclair clenched his jaw. "Fucking bastard!"

"And I enjoyed every second of it," Liam said.

"Are you gonna kill us?" I asked.

Mr. Sinclair sneered. "No, I've got something worse in mind. I'm taking Liam home."

"What?" Liam exclaimed.

Mr. Sinclair shifted his weight. "Give the faggot your keys, Liam. He can take your car home, and you can get it back from him later."

My throat burned. I didn't care about Mr. Sinclair, so I shouldn't have been bothered by what he said about me—not even for a second. Yet I almost screamed into the couch pillow. It was as if Mr. Sinclair didn't even think I was human.

"If you don't leave with me, then I'm gonna press charges over him attacking me," Mr. Sinclair said. "I presume he told you about our altercation."

Only a moron would've overplayed their hand. So I couldn't say anything about having Mr. Sinclair's confession. Not yet. That was my only trump card, and I had to be absolutely certain when I used it.

I swallowed hard, torn between wanting to be brave for Liam and concern over the consequences Liam would face at home. "It's okay, Liam."

"Are you sure?" Liam's eyebrows were furrowed, and his eyes were wide underneath them.

"Yes," I said.

"Okay." Liam tossed me his car keys before his father yanked him away by the shirt collar, dragging him outside.

Damn. So much for us enjoying a romantic weekend alone. Of course, the universe just had to mess with our lives.

Tears dotted my eyes. Sometimes the greatest acts of violence didn't actually involve violence. Liam must've died a little every time Mr. Sinclair was so cruel. And if I wanted to save both Liam and our relationship, then I needed to figure out how to leverage that confession against Mr. Sinclair. I didn't care if it was the last thing I did. Mr. Sinclair was gonna pay for his misdeeds.

CHAPTER 24

Liam approached me at school the next day. He greeted me with a hug instead of his usual quick kiss.

"Hi," he said, pulling away a moment later.

"Sorry I didn't text or stop by your house," I said. "I didn't wanna make the situation worse for you."

"No apology needed. Just got my phone back this morning."

"Your father didn't beat the shit out of you, did he?" I asked.

"Nope."

"For real?"

"He was nice to me for the whole weekend."

"That's good. At least, I think it is."

"He says we can keep dating," Liam said.

I stared. "What happened to him being the biggest homophobe in history?"

Liam slouched. "Maybe he feels guilty about killing Evelyn. Stranger things have happened."

"Tell me exactly what he said."

"He wants to 'end this cycle of violence,'" Liam said. "Something about not wanting anything to interrupt his drinking."

Cycle of violence. It was an interesting choice of words. If Liam hadn't paraphrased Mr. Sinclair's response, and his father had used that exact phrasing, then he was aware of how shitty a person he was. Even if only on a subconscious level.

I forced a laugh. "Never thought I'd be thankful for someone's drinking problem."

"We're gonna be okay."

"Do you believe him?" I asked.

"Doesn't matter. I meant what I said before. I'm not letting my father steal one more thing from me."

I smiled at him. "Fair enough."

Liam lowered his head, remaining silent. Poor guy. I still didn't know what kind of person I'd have been if I grew up in the environment Liam had. It was a miracle Liam wasn't more fucked up than he already was. A toxic home life would've pushed me over the edge.

"There's something we should talk about," Liam said. "We were having a heated conversation when my father showed up."

Crap. I guessed the universe's benevolence couldn't extend to other areas of my life. I didn't have memory problems—I knew I'd asked whether Liam was with me out of desperation for someone to love him.

A few students darted by while the chatter around us grew louder and louder. A gust of wind nipped at our faces when a teacher entered the building through the side entrance.

"I'm sorry for what I said, and I understand if you wanna break up with me," I said. "You deserve someone who supports you no matter what."

He whipped his head vigorously. "Enough."

"Excuse me?"

"Why do you think I'm gonna break up with you whenever we disagree?" Liam asked.

"I don't know."

"I have an idea. And I think you probably understand your behavior on some level, but I'm not gonna tell you how to feel."

Interesting. Liam could've told me what he thought motivated my behavior, but he knew the realization wouldn't have any impact on me unless I uncovered it myself.

I didn't need more time to figure out what Liam was referring to, though. Anyone with half a brain could infer that Liam wasn't the only one in pain. I still carried my father's death around with me. And him dying had to be why I always worried about the universe taking things from me. If Dad could die unexpectedly, then anything was possible.

"You don't have to say anything," I said.

"Figured it out?" Liam asked.

"Yup."

"You can talk about it if you want."

The bell rang, and more students scurried by. A poster hanging on an adjacent wall by a single piece of tape fell onto the ground.

"I'm good," I said.

Liam sighed. "I still gotta get my car back."

Thank goodness he didn't press the issue further. School wasn't the place to discuss my insecurities about Dad's death. Plus, acceptance worked both ways. If I had to deal with Liam's imperfections, then he needed to tolerate mine. Fair was fair. I'd chat about my issues when the time was right.

I fixed my shirt collar. "I can drive you back to my house after school and then you can take your car home."

"I have practice."

"I can go to Starbucks while you're there."

He wiggled his eyebrows. "Don't wanna watch me practice football for an hour?"

"Not really."

Liam put his hand over his chest. "I'm crushed."

I chuckled. "I'm sure you'll find some way to live."

The following morning before first period, I bumped into Evan and Jordon in the hallway.

"Thank goodness we found you," Jordon said.

I shot Jordon an inquisitive look. "Something wrong?"

"Did you see the local news this morning?" Evan asked.

I locked my arms together. "No. Why?"

"Liam has been arrested," Evan said.

My eyes almost popped out of their sockets. The blood in my body felt like it had dropped about twenty degrees in temperature. "For what?"

"Attempting to murder his father," Jordon blurted.

I passed a hand over my eyes. "Fuck," I said under my breath.

Evan patted my shoulder. "Whatever you and Liam need, just name it."

"Evan is right," Jordon said.

"How did Liam's arrest even leak?" I asked, still trying to process the information. "He's a minor."

Evan pulled his backpack strap up. "Maybe his father is responsible."

"Mr. Sinclair must know influential people," Jordon said.

"True," I said.

Evan winced. "I'm glad I'm not Liam. I wouldn't wanna be in jail—even if it's only county jail."

Damn. So much for the cycle of violence ending. There were a thousand things I would've rather done than start Tuesday morning with my boyfriend being arrested. If this was how the beginning of the week was going, then I didn't wanna think about how the rest of the week might unfold.

CHAPTER 25

I sat across from Liam at a table in the Greenwood County Jail visitor's room after school. Apparently, in some states, minors could sometimes be placed in County Jail as opposed to Juvie—Liam was seventeen, not sixteen.

Liam sported an orange short-sleeved shirt and matching pants, and both his hands and ankles were handcuffed. A guard stood at the door a few feet away, but we had the room to ourselves—there were no other prisoners or visitors in the vicinity.

"It's good to see you," I said.

Liam scoffed. "I don't even know why you came. This is your fault."

"That's a little harsh."

"My father changed a few facts, but he's blaming me for what you did the night of my away football game."

"How? His bruises are healed."

"He took photos and gave a very detailed statement to the police."

"Attempted murder is a stretch," I said, eyebrows raised. "Especially the District Attorney wanting to try you as an adult."

"I'm never gonna forgive you for this—you had no right interfering in my life. And you've got no idea what being here is like. Wondering if someone is gonna kill me."

Ouch. Someone stabbing me with a knife wouldn't have hurt as much as Liam's comment. Not being perfect didn't mean my intentions were bad. They weren't. But I'd need to consider my actions more carefully in the future.

"I'm sorry, Liam," I said. "I never wanted this. I didn't think anything bad was gonna happen."

Liam glared, his eyes icy. "That's your problem, Connor. You don't think. Being with you is the worst thing that's ever happened to me. My life would be so much simpler if I'd just kept pretending I was straight."

"You don't mean that."

"I do."

"I can use the recording to blackmail your father into dropping the charges," I said.

"I don't want you to do anything—you'll make everything fucking worse," Liam barked. "Fucking life up is your specialty."

Maybe Liam was doing me a favor with his response. Our relationship would never work as long as his father remained an obstacle. I couldn't afford to get more invested if we'd never have a real future.

"What happened to you? I thought you loved me."

"Wasn't real," Liam muttered. "Just desperate to think it was."

"Don't be like this."

"Just leave! The guard's probably gonna come get me in a minute."

"You never told me how much the bail is."

Liam's gaze moved to the floor. "$500,000."

I spun around in the school hallway the next day after sipping water from the water fountain, only to find Mona, Natalie, and Gavin in front of me.

"We wanted to see how you were doing. After… everything," Natalie said.

"Please let us know if we can do anything for you," Gavin chimed in.

I wiped water from my lip. "Thanks."

"We're serious," Mona said.

My eyes started to burn. "Liam and I might be done."

"What are you talking about?" Gavin asked.

I averted my gaze while shame crept through my body. "Long story, but I messed things up."

Mona furrowed her brows. "Can you improve the situation somehow?"

"I could," I said.

Mona blinked. "How?"

"I can pay Liam's bail. I don't have access to my college savings account, but I've got the funds to pay it because of the money my father left me. $500,000 to be exact."

"You'd sacrifice your entire inheritance?" Mona asked.

Mona could lose the shock. I'd survive without the money Dad had left me—I'd find another way to remember him. If the inheritance could do something good, then I didn't have a choice in the matter.

"Liam doesn't deserve to rot in jail for a problem I caused," I said.

Gavin clapped my back. "I'm sure that'd mean a lot to him."

Liam shifted his head while he sat in the front passenger seat of my Mercedes and I made a left.

"Thanks for paying my bail," Liam said, voice quiet.

"No problem."

"I'll pay you back. I promise."

"We both know you won't, and that's okay." I honked my car horn at a deer, and it crossed the street. "You didn't tell me where you want me to drop you off. Can I bring you to Evan's house, Jordon's?"

"No."

"You don't wanna go back to your house?"

He extended his arm, then caressed my knee. "I want to spend the night with you."

"You don't owe me anything. I would've helped out any friend."

"I don't wanna be alone," Liam said.

"Okay."

Liam leaned forward, right hand tucked under the side of his head while we laid in my bed hours later. He flashed his usual post-sex smirk.

"Glad you enjoyed yourself," I said before resting my head on the pillow behind me.

"Hope you did, too."

"What are we doing, Liam?" I asked.

"You're still my boyfriend—not like we actually ended things."

"You were pretty angry."

He sniffed. "People say things they don't mean all the time."

"Okay."

"You really are the only good thing in my life."

"I've cost you everything."

"But you made me wanna become a better person, and I owe you everything for that."

I closed my eyes instead of responding. History was once again repeating itself. Mr. Sinclair was a prick, and we couldn't do anything about it. And my bedroom was still our own little world, because it was the only place Liam, and I were safe.

CHAPTER 26

"Sorry for the stealth meeting—discretion's kind of best right now," Liam said.

We stood in an empty school hallway a week after I'd paid his bail, and my blood was burning through my body. Nothing worse than not being in control of a situation. I had no idea why Liam wanted to talk.

"No worries," I said.

He let out a long breath. "I wanna break up with you for real this time."

I blinked. I felt like the floor had just collapsed under me. "Are you kidding?"

"Nope. I'm serious."

"Every couple fights—it's normal. Not like it turned into violence or something."

"It's not about that."

"I'm really not mad at you for punching me last spring."

"Not that, either."

I put my hands on my hips. "Then what?"

"My father will drop the charges if I break up with you."

What a coward. What a damn coward. Liam would always be the person who chose to save himself over doing the right thing, and I couldn't believe I hadn't realized that before now. Only a fool would've continued to make excuses because of how attractive someone was.

"What the hell?" I was almost unable to breathe.

"Not the best course of action. But I gotta do what I gotta do."

"Our relationship must not have been worth shit to you." I fought back the tears. No way I'd let myself be hurt by this arrogant, dipshit jock. My courage wasn't something Liam or anyone else could take.

Liam didn't speak.

"I can use the recording to blackmail your father to drop the charges," I said. "But you're probably just looking for an out."

"Don't say that."

"You never loved me. Admit it."

Liam grabbed my hands. "Doesn't have to be like this forever. Just for a little while."

"What do you mean?" I demanded.

"I've got a plan."

"And what's that?"

"I can't tell you."

What a joke. Liam had harped about how secrets were poisonous before, and now he was keeping a huge one from me. Obviously, he didn't care about seeming hypocritical. It was kind of lazy of him. Liam would've tried hiding his less favorable personality traits if he actually cared about me.

"You're full of shit." I kicked my sneakers against the tile floor. "God. I wasted so much time on you. I knew you were trouble, but I got involved with you anyway. Guess I liked playing with fire."

"Connor, please!" Liam exclaimed.

"Wanna know something? The sex wasn't that good."

"Now I know you're lying."

"You will always be a terrible fucking person, Liam Sinclair!" I screamed. "And you know what? I hope your father kills you. It's what you deserve after all the times you manipulated me into thinking your feelings were real."

His Adam's apple bobbed. "You've got no reason to believe me, but it wasn't all a lie with you."

Please. Nothing Liam could say would change my opinion of him now. What was done was done, and he needed to leave me alone. Some people just weren't capable of changing.

I suppressed more tears. "Get out of my sight."

"Let's talk about this," Liam said.

"Nothing to discuss. You're a typical fuckboy."

He rolled up the sleeves of his plaid flannel button-down. "That's not fair."

"Newsflash. Life isn't fair."

A tear rolled down his cheek. "You're a great guy, and I hope you get everything you want out of life. You deserve it."

Empty words from an empty guy. If Liam wanted to impress me, then he would've revealed something deeper. Something I didn't know—something that made his pain palpable the way the photos for my art gallery debut had.

I sobbed on Gavin's knee while he sat up on my living room couch.

Gavin patted my shoulder. "Might seem meaningless saying this now, but your bad luck will change. Just give it time."

I lifted my head from Gavin's knee, then grabbed a tissue and blew my nose. "Sorry for getting so emotional."

"It's called being human."

"Nice of you to say."

"If you it makes you feel better, I don't think Liam is completely full of shit. He was very unhappy before meeting you."

"Thanks." My iPhone vibrated and I whipped it out of my pocket. "Hello?"

"It's Liam."

"I know. You're still on my contacts."

Liam coughed, creating brief static on his end.

"You called me," I reminded him.

"Right," Liam said. "I wasn't being honest with you earlier today. I'm ready to tell you everything now. Can you be at my house in fifteen minutes?"

Liam had to be joking. One minute he wanted to end our relationship, and the next he wanted to chat. If I didn't know better, I would've thought my life was a soap opera. I could only handle so much drama, and could only pray my life would get simpler ASAP.

I rolled my eyes even though Liam couldn't see it. "I'm hanging with Gavin."

"He can come," Liam said.

"Fine."

"Great. See you soon."

I pressed 'end' on my iPhone, then tossed it onto the coffee table.

"It's good Liam called you," Gavin said.

"I guess."

"Do you wanna drive, or should I?"

"You can drive, if you don't mind." I scratched my scalp. "I'm not in the right frame of my mind."

"No problem."

I screamed when Gavin and I entered Liam's unlocked house. Blood coated the wall and floor near the front door.

My heart almost leapt out my chest. The amount of blood… it seemed impossible anyone could survive that much blood loss.

"Liam!" Gavin roared.

No answer.

Gavin screamed even louder this time. "Liam!"

Nobody walked over to us.

Gavin eyed me for a sec. "Stay right here. I'm gonna check the rest of the house."

"Okay."

"I can't find him anywhere," Gavin returned to me sometime later.

"I'll say it if you won't. Do you think Liam is dead?" I asked.

"I don't know." Gavin tucked his hands into his jeans' pockets. "But we should call the police."

Gavin had a point. There was nothing else we could do—we were only teenagers, and this situation was best left to the proper authorities.

"What if his father killed him?" I asked.

"Then Mona, Natalie, and I will support you with whatever you need."

Gavin pulled out his iPhone while my chest expanded and contracted, my breathing becoming more rapid. Killing one child was bad enough, but if Mr. Sinclair had murdered Liam, too, then he was an even bigger monster than I'd realized.

I couldn't help feeling incredibly guilty. I should've handled Liam's home life better. Like panicking more, protecting Liam, or removing him from his bad situation. It wasn't like I didn't care, though. I was still just a kid. If I pushed too much, then I could've alienated Liam, which would've further isolated him. And Liam was the athletic one, not me. If he couldn't deal with his father effectively, then there wasn't much hope for me handling Mr. Sinclair. Fuck. I couldn't believe how complicated life had gotten since junior year began. Life wasn't supposed to be so serious at my age. The person I cared about most in the world was probably dead, and there wasn't a fucking thing I could about it.

CHAPTER 27

My doorbell rang several afternoons after discovering the blood at Liam's house. I opened my door—Gavin stood on the front porch with a folded piece of paper in his right hand.

"Hi, man," he said.

"What's up?"

"Can I come in?"

"Sure." I shut the door behind Gavin.

"Doing this in private is best."

"What are you talking about?" I asked.

"Liam wrote you a letter when he was released on bail and asked me to give it to you if something happened to him."

"Are you saying he knew his father was gonna kill him?"

Gavin shrugged. "Maybe."

"Why would you wait until now to give me this?"

"His death was just ruled a homicide yesterday." Gavin handed me the paper. "If you want, I can go."

Homicide. It was hard to grasp Gavin using that word in reference to Liam. Yet here I was, faced with Liam's death. Apparently, the police ruled deaths homicide even if a body was never discovered. It would've been nice if the police had tried harder to look for Liam. But no. According to the police, the amount of blood lost made it unlikely that Liam was still alive. Fucking unbelievable. Just like that, Liam was dead.

"Would you mind staying?" I asked, starting to shake a little. "I don't feel like being alone."

"Sure."

Thank goodness he'd agreed to stay. I didn't know what I would do if I had to read the letter alone. This letter was my last link to Liam, and he'd really be dead once I finished studying it.

I unfolded the letter after taking several deep breaths.

Dear Connor,

If you're reading this, my father has probably killed me. But please don't be miserable about it. The time I spent with you has been the best time of my life. Our relationship might not have been perfect, but you gave me two things I never thought I'd experience. Being loved and the ability to love.

The next days won't be easy for you, but eventually, you'll need to move on with your life.

Love,

Liam

The letter fell to the ground and my crying mixed with screams. Gavin opened his arms, inviting me in for a hug. He rubbed my back while I sobbed louder and louder. No amount of time would make the universe's latest theft okay. Liam was dead, just like Dad and Evelyn. The only guarantee I had now was that the empty feeling in my stomach was going to keep expanding. Tragedy had no positive spin.

"He's really gone," I said.

"I know, I know."

"Here." Mom handed me a cup of coffee the following morning while we sat in the kitchen.

"Thanks." I sipped at it and then placed it on the kitchen counter.

"I'm glad I caught an earlier flight."

"You didn't have to."

Mom put a hand on my shoulder. "Don't be ridiculous. Traveling doesn't mean I don't care about what you're going through."

"Kind of ironic."

"What do you mean?" she asked.

"Ruling Liam's death a murder because of all the blood loss but eliminating Mr. Sinclair as a suspect because he had an alibi—drinking at a fucking a bar. Security cameras even confirm it."

Mom took her glasses off, then wiped them with a cloth. "Do you wanna skip school today? Maybe see a movie and go out to lunch?"

"Nothing matters at this point," I said.

"Remember something."

"And what's that?"

"Your relationship with Liam was real, no matter how vile Mr. Sinclair was." Mom brushed a piece of hair out of my face. "Please never forget that."

She was right. Even if Mr. had Sinclair muddied my relationship my relationship with Liam, he couldn't take my memories of the time we'd spent together. So, I'd have the last laugh. Liam had got to live his truth as a gay guy, and that was what mattered.

"I'm gonna attend Liam's funeral. Mr. Sinclair be damned."

Mom rubbed her forehead.

"He can't keep me from saying my final goodbye," I said, filled with a sudden ferocity. "I'll fucking kill him if he does."

"I wouldn't expect anything less. But let's hope it doesn't come to murder."

I shuffled through the hallway half an hour later, tears forming in my eyes. I ran to the nearest bathroom, then rushed to the sink, head down.

I cried. And cried. And cried. Liam had been my first relationship, and I couldn't shrug that loss off. I was also mourning the life he'd never have. A life that the universe had stolen from him when his only crime was having Mr. Sinclair as a father.

The door opened, and two hands touched my back. I lifted my gaze from the sink. Evan and Jordon stood behind me.

"We're so sorry for your loss," Evan said.

I assumed a fetal position, and Evan and Jordon squatted next to me.

"If you think Mr. Sinclair is responsible for Liam's death, then we'll help you prove it. If that's what you want," Jordon said.

"Absolutely," Evan reiterated.

"Thanks. I appreciate that." I rubbed my eyes with my shirt. "But first I've gotta get through Liam's funeral."

"We can go with you if you want," Evan said.

Evan and Jordon's kindness meant more to me than they realized. They couldn't solve my problems or erase my grief, but their presence was enough to let me know I wasn't alone. The real tragedy would've been not having anyone there to support me.

"Yeah, I might need you two." I chuckled without any humor. "No telling what kind of mood Mr. Sinclair will be in at the funeral."

Evan sighed. "Also, we wanted to apologize."

I quirked my eyebrows. "For what?"

Jordon's jaw twitched. "For last May. We should've handled Liam better when he went ballistic."

"Why apologize now?" I asked.

Evan shrugged. "Better late than never."

"True." I nodded, suppressing my urge to snicker. Laugher didn't seem appropriate. Not when Liam was dead. "Anyway, apology accepted."

"Thanks for not giving us a hard time," Evan said.

I inhaled a deep breath. "Nobody is perfect."

I meant what I said. If I felt like being a dick, then I could've tossed their apology back in their faces. But being a jackass wouldn't change anything. The palpable dread from Liam's death would still exist. The punishment also needed to fit the crime. Evan and Jordon might've behaved like cowards that day last May, but they were still teenagers. If they wanted a chance to change, then they deserved the opportunity.

Jordon gave me a sympathetic look. "You really don't have to go through this alone. Evan and I are serious about supporting you."

"Thanks," I whispered.

CHAPTER 28

Natalie, Mona, Gavin, Evan, Jordon, and I stood at the edge of the parking lot Saturday morning. Mr. Sinclair was alone on the sidewalk by the church's front. Gray clouds dotted the sky, and a light drizzle pattered against the ground.

"I should greet Mr. Sinclair. That'd be the polite thing to do," I said.

Jordon bit his lip. "That might not be the best idea, man."

"Not like we're gonna kill each other in public." I shuffled over to Mr. Sinclair, whose gaze was buried in his iPhone. "I'm sorry for your loss."

He looked up at me. "What are you doing here, faggot?"

"Really gonna make a scene at your son's funeral?" I asked. "Seems beneath even you."

He clenched his teeth. "I won't make a fuss."

Time to alert every media outlet in the country. Never thought I'd be able to reason with a brick wall. Worse than a brick wall, because a wall wouldn't talk back. There was no telling what Mr. Sinclair's next move would be.

"Good." I spread my arms. "Why don't you bring it in for a quick hug? Don't worry. Not like I'm gonna kiss you. I wouldn't touch your lips with a ten-foot pole."

"Fine. Good PR never hurts." Mr. Sinclair obliged me.

I leaned towards his right ear. "I recorded your confession from that night, and I'm gonna make you pay for Evelyn's death if it's the last thing I do. And don't bother destroying my iPhone. I already emailed the recording to multiple email addresses."

"What the fuck are you talking about?"

"Your luck is running out. I'm gonna take you down once and for all." I stepped away from Mr. Sinclair. "But enjoy Liam's funeral. Maybe it'll be a good opportunity to reflect on what a terrible father you were."

"You've got some nerve," Mr. Sinclair said, face growing bright red.

A group of people walked by us, then entered the church. The parking lot was getting more and more crowded. There were almost no free spots left, which would've made me smile if I wasn't talking to Mr. Sinclair. Liam deserved a packed church for his funeral. This was the last time anyone but me would give a shit about him, and he needed to go out with a bang.

"I'm not afraid of you," I said.

"You should be."

"Why? Are you in the mood to add a third murder to your list?" I demanded.

"I didn't kill Liam," Mr. Sinclair mumbled, almost slurring his words.

"Bullshit."

Our group sat toward the back of the church sometime later while the pastor babbled on and on with his eulogy. My spine tingled. There was something weird about seeing the gigantic blown-up photo of Liam to the right of the pastor. It was almost like he was a celebrity.

Mom was right about one thing, though. Mr. Sinclair couldn't deprive me of the good times I'd shared with Liam. No matter how painful dwelling on Liam was, I'd have to do my best to remember the positive times. Those the moments with Liam were the only thing I had left of him.

I sat at Liam's lunch table with him, Evan, Jordon, and his other football friends. We'd just started dating but including me in his world was a good first step.

Timothy—the guy with a buzz-cut sitting at the end of the table—looked my way. "What do you like to do for fun, Connor?"

"Besides Liam," Jordon said.

Getting angry would've been the easy response. But rage didn't flare through my body. The joke might've been Jordon's way of letting Liam know he was okay with his sexuality. And anyway, it wasn't a stretch to imagine they made racy jokes all the time. They were teenagers, after all.

Evan gave Jordon a disapproving look.

"I had to go for it—it was right there," Jordon said.

I chugged the rest of my chocolate milk. "I like photography."

Timothy laughed. "Great. Maybe you can take some photos of Liam at some point."

I paused in preparing dinner to answer the door one evening. Liam stood on my front porch with a pizza box. Rain was pummeling the ground, getting louder with each passing second.

"Did I miss a text?" I asked.

"Nope."

"Then what's the occasion?"

"Trying to cheer you up because none of your photos sold at the art gallery debut." Liam held the pizza box closer to his chest.

"Thanks," I said.

"Don't mention it."

Wow. I might've had the best boyfriend in the world. The gesture wasn't something I would've expected from Liam. I hadn't complained too much about not selling any of my photos the night I debuted. Art, including photography, was subjective. I'd also have other chances to sell my art. One failed opportunity wasn't the end of the world.

"May I come in?" he asked.

I chuckled. "Yeah. You've gotten wet enough."

Liam yawned and stretched his arms while morning sunlight poked through my bedroom curtains.

"Morning," I said.

"Let's skip school today and spend the whole day in bed. Not like we'll use any of that bullshit in real life."

"If you skip school, then you can't go to football practice."

He jabbed his fist through the air. "Fucking shit."

"How about a compromise?" I asked. "Ten more minutes before we start getting ready?"

Liam waggled his eyebrows. "Perfect."

I scooted toward Liam, then let my head collapse onto his chest. His fingers snaked through my hair and I closed my eyes. We didn't have all the time in the world, but we were making time for us, and that was what counted.

The echoing sound of the harp a musician was plucking at the front of the church snapped me out of my reminiscence.

Tears formed in my eyes, but I didn't wipe them away.

I would've given almost anything to get back those ten minutes that Liam and I had taken for ourselves before dragging our lazy asses out of bed.

Gavin leaned closer to me. "Are you okay?"

"No."

He squeezed my knee while the harpist continued playing, and I closed my eyes. Liam Sinclair—the boy I loved—was really dead. No redoes. No surprise plot twist. Nobody saying this was only a prank. Nope. There was only my pain, and I had no fucking clue how I was supposed to live on with it. Teenagers weren't supposed to experience three deaths in one year. It was just too cruel.

So, yeah. I might not have figured out the specific details yet, but there was a good chance Mr. Sinclair, and I were gonna have another confrontation. Evelyn's and Liam's deaths were his fault, and he was gonna pay with his life.

CHAPTER 29

I banged on Liam's front door several times. I'd done the same the evening before, but Mr. Sinclair had refused to answer the door for me.

My teeth chattered from the chill permeating the air. It was hard to believe fall was already well established and winter would arrive soon. Seemed like yesterday Liam had been apologizing to me after my salon appointment.

I paced back and forth on Liam's front porch. Chatting with Mr. Sinclair would require more patience than I probably had. But the task had to be done. The conflict between us was gonna end one way or another, because my mind hadn't changed since Liam's funeral. His father needed to pay for every horrible thing he'd done.

An animal howled, and I almost jumped. It sounded like a coyote had just attacked a deer.

I made a fist, then knocked on the front door several more times.

The door opened. Mr. Sinclair stood in the entryway, looming and shadow eyed.

"What are you doing here?" he asked in a gravelly voice.

"We need to talk." I didn't wait for an invitation, barging into the house.

Mr. Sinclair followed me into his living room.

"Can I get you a drink?" Mr. Sinclair offered. The politeness was dripping with insincerity.

"No, thanks. I shouldn't drink and drive."

"How responsible."

My gaze shifted. A half-empty bottle of whiskey was on the coffee table.

"Live a little—only young once," he said.

"I didn't drop by to discuss booze."

"Then what do you want?" Mr. Sinclair slurred his words together.

"I want you to do something for me."

"You've gotta be fucking kidding me."

"It's only you and me here, and I'm not recording you like I did when you confessed to Evelyn's murder."

"You haven't told me what you want."

"Confess to killing Liam. It'll be our secret."

He lunged forward, smacking his index finger against my chest. "How many times do I have to tell you that I didn't murder Liam? But I guess you're too dense, too much of a fucking moron faggot."

"Yes, I know you have an alibi."

"You're wasting my time, then." Mr. Sinclair made a swipe at the table and chugged whiskey from his bottle.

Good gracious. It was a miracle that Mr. Sinclair's liver hadn't exploded from all the booze he consumed. He made college and partying as a twenty-something look G-rated. And I would've bet my life that Mr. Sinclair would finish off the remainder of his whiskey by the end of the evening. If I didn't finish him first, that was. No telling what might happen between us. Liam was dead, but I couldn't be at peace until I found a permanent solution to Mr. Sinclair.

"You could've paid someone to kill Liam," I said.

He cackled. "Even you can't be stupid enough to think that."

"Come again?" I asked.

"If I wanted Liam dead, I'd have killed him myself."

"Do you care that Liam is gone?" I demanded.

"What kind of question is that?" Mr. Sinclair whipped his body around to face me. "Being a fucking faggot doesn't change the fact he was my son."

"I want something else from you."

"What?" Mr. Sinclair spat.

"Did you have a crappy childhood?" I asked. "Maybe your parents physically, sexually, emotionally abused you?"

I didn't want to find out about Mr. Sinclair's upbringing because I gave a shit about him—I didn't. I just had to know what motivated him to be so cruel. An explanation was the least I deserved after everything Liam and I had endured because of him.

He expelled a hyena laugh. "No. They gave me everything I wanted."

"Something is seriously fucked up about you," I tried again. "You couldn't have learned this behavior by yourself."

His nostrils flared. "I'm just a miserable son of a bitch. I learned a long time that you can either push people around or be the one who gets pushed around—no question which option's the smarter one."

"Unbelievable."

"Tell me something. How does it feel knowing you'll never see Liam again?" Mr. Sinclair let out a rattling chuckle. "Your pain is the only thing getting me through."

"Are you fucking kidding me?"

"You were the worst thing that ever happened to him. You turned him into an abomination."

"We were in love."

Mr. Sinclair smirked. "Liam was confused, and I could've helped him. Turned him into a real man."

"Why do you just… hate gay people?" I was unable to swallow the lump in my throat.

"Goes against the natural order of life."

"And who made you the morality police?"

"Leave!" Mr. Sinclair spat, fists clenching. "You prevented my son from living his true potential. I never wanna see your dumb faggot ass again."

I screamed as thoughts swirled through my mind. Thoughts about how Liam and I would never see each other again, let alone have another date or be intimate. About how we wouldn't attend Junior or Senior Prom. Or graduate high school together. Or even be able to think about a future after high school.

Mr. Sinclair's ghoulish smile hadn't disappeared, so I yelled even louder. Mr. Sinclair might not have killed Liam, but he'd enjoyed making Liam miserable, and he enjoyed how my grief was suffocating me, how I would have to struggle through the impossibility of life without Liam.

So I had one option. It was time to do what I'd come here to do. Mr. Sinclair had no redeeming qualities, no matter how much I wished he did.

I pulled the cake knife from my jacket pocket, then shoved it into Mr. Sinclair's stomach as deep as I could. He collapsed onto the carpet. A steady stream of blood spilled out of his mouth and onto the soft beige covering the floor, staining it red.

Mr. Sinclair gripped his chest, then the light went out in his eyes.

The doorbell rang.

My hands started shaking. I couldn't believe it—I'd killed Mr. Sinclair.

The doorbell sounded several more times.

I looked through the peephole on the front door. Violet stood on the porch.

She knocked on the door several more times.

Shit. Well, Violet probably wasn't going to turn me in.

I opened it, then gesticulated at her. "Come in quickly."

Violet entered the house, and I locked the door behind her.

She glanced at my T-shirt, then made eye contact. "Why are you covered in blood?"

"It's complicated," I said.

She bit her lip. "I promise not to judge no matter how bad the situation is. You were honest with me that night at the party, so I'll give you the same courtesy."

I wiped tears from my eyes—not considering that I might be accidentally smearing Mr. Sinclair's blood across my face until afterward. My pulse soared. "I killed Mr. Sinclair in cold blood. I'm gonna have to go to prison for the rest of my life," I said.

Violet shook her head. "You aren't. We're gonna find a way out of this."

Surprise flooded my body. It was great that Violet wanted to help me, yet I would've expected her to make a big deal about Mr. Sinclair's death. I guessed things were a little different when you murdered a murderer.

CHAPTER 30

I made a brief fist. "You don't have to help me, Violet. I fucked up, and Mr. Sinclair's death is my responsibility to deal with."

She giggled. "Don't act like I'm perfect."

"Excuse me?"

"You weren't the only one who came here to kill him."

"Huh?" I asked, still confused. Violet couldn't have meant that. Two people showing up at Mr. Sinclair's house to kill him at the same time seemed highly unlikely.

She tugged at her pigtail. "I wanted justice for Evelyn."

Wow. Life was getting stranger and stranger. Really, though, I shouldn't have been shocked. A terrible person like Mr. Sinclair would have a lot of enemies. Plenty of people might've wanted him dead.

"After what she did?" I asked.

"Still my best friend."

"There's no way I'm gonna get away with this." I stared at the floor. "My fingerprints are on the cake knife—I brought it from my house."

Violet exhaled a breath. "Just take the cake knife with you and wipe your prints off it."

"Okay." I probably should've been able to think of that myself, but I was still shaken up.

"We should call your friends."

My head almost detached from my neck. "No offense, but have you lost your damn mind? More people will only complicate this."

"Can't deal with it alone."

"Fine."

"And you're gonna need to wipe the blood off your face."

Shit. So it *had* gotten on me. Although a messy face was the least of my problems.

"You don't have to baby me," I said sometime later. I was standing next to Gavin in front of Liam's sink.

"It's fine."

I splashed cold water onto my face, wiping away the blood. I let the faucet run a little longer than I should've. I was paranoid about leaving any traces of blood in the sink.

"Take your shirt off," Gavin said.

"Come again?"

"You've gotta change your shirt and burn the one you have on." Gavin waved his T-shirt at me. "Remember? I brought a fresh one for you."

I touched my right cheek. "Sorry."

"Don't apologize to me. I'm not the one who got stabbed."

I gave him a venomous look.

"I'm kidding," Gavin amended quickly.

I removed my leather jacket—which somehow hadn't gotten any blood on it—before taking off my old T-shirt and slipping into a new one.

Gavin gave me a small smile. "Everything will be fine, Connor."

Footsteps echoed, then Violet, Evan, Jordon, Natalie, and Mona entered the kitchen.

"Everything okay?" Violet asked.

"Yeah. I'll take Connor home so we can burn his old shirt," Gavin said.

I cleared my throat before looking everyone in the eye, one at a time. "Helping me means more than you'll ever know. Some people might say I'm as bad as Mr. Sinclair."

"Not true," Jordon said.

Evan nodded. "He's right."

I looked at my shoes. "It was premeditated murder."

"Everyone makes mistakes," Natalie said.

Mona rubbed at the gold bracelet looped around her right wrist. "Even me."

"You're lucky Liam gave you the combination to his mother's safe. We can leave a few pieces of jewelry by his body and then take the rest," Violet said.

"Don't forget moving the furniture and making a mess." Mona crossed her arms. "If we want the living room to look like a robbery gone bad, then we need to create the right conditions."

My head throbbed. The pieces of our cover up were falling into place easier than a jigsaw puzzle. And I didn't know if I should be relieved, terrified, or both. This was the last thing that should've happened to us this year. But here I was, about to get away with murder.

"You might've gotten your prints everywhere," I said.

"We'll be fine. None of us have criminal records," Evan waved me off.

"If you say so. Anyway, who has the cake knife?"

"I washed it in the bathroom sink." Jordon handed me the knife and the jewelry we'd "stolen."

"Thanks," I said.

"Do me a favor. Don't stab anyone else tonight." He smirked.

Violet gave him a look.

Jordon put his hands up. "I was joking."

"Why am I keeping the valuables?" I asked.

"You were his boyfriend, and you might need the money someday," Violet said. "But you might wanna wait before selling them. Like, a few months."

"Who do you think is gonna find the body?" Evan asked.

"The maid usually comes tomorrow," I said.

Mona glanced out the window. "Well, at least you parked around the corner so nobody can claim they saw your Mercedes in the driveway."

"Thanks again for everything, you guys."

Gavin put his arm around me. "Enough formalities."

Gavin and I sat in my living room sometime later.

Flames illuminated the fireplace, swallowing my T-shirt while the crackling grew louder and louder.

"You didn't have to stay with me," I said.

"Not good for you to be alone."

I frowned. "I'm not gonna hurt myself."

"That's not my concern."

"Then what?"

"You killed someone," Gavin said.

"No shit."

"My point is you were put in an impossible situation."

"I hope nobody thinks I'm a terrible person for what I did," I said.

"They don't."

"You sure about that?"

"If you go down, then everyone else is finished, too," Gavin said.

I didn't respond. Instead, Gavin's response lingered in my mind. He was right, morbid as his comment was. We would all be bound together for the rest of our lives because of what had happened this evening. And I wasn't sure how to feel about that beyond the obvious gratitude. Six other people meant six variables besides myself, and I could only hope Gavin was right and they wouldn't crack under pressure.

Killing Mr. Sinclair didn't mean the rest of my life was ruined, though. Murder was wrong, generally, yet I wouldn't budge on my opinion. I was owed a free murder after the universe had cut Liam's life short.

I sat on a stool in my kitchen several mornings later while an omelet sizzled in the frying pan—Mom wanted to make me breakfast. Apparently, she also wanted to talk.

Mom turned away from the stove. "I found the cake knife in a different drawer than I usually keep it in."

"Oh?"

"I needed a knife to cut the pound cake I bought yesterday."

"I see."

"I also heard about Mr. Sinclair's death on the news."

Damn. Mr. Sinclair was ruining my life even when he was dead. I didn't need to discuss him while having breakfast before school. He was occupying enough of my headspace already, and I needed to move on with my life.

"If you're gonna accuse me of something, then be more specific. I'm not gonna be treated like a criminal in my own home."

"I'm not saying you did anything." Mom scooped the cheese omelet onto a plate, then handed it to me before pushing ketchup and a glass of water over.

"Then what?" I asked.

Mom bit her lip. "Are you gonna need a lawyer?"

"I took care of it."

She gripped her hair. "And what does that mean?"

"Do you wanna know the truth?" I broke off a piece of omelet, then dunked it in ketchup. "I'll tell you. But then you're gonna have to live knowing what I did."

Mom raised her palm at me. "No. If you really killed Mr. Sinclair, I'm not going to turn you into the police."

"They ruled his death a robbery gone bad," I said. "Probably never find the culprit."

"And I'm a Vanderbilt."

Thank goodness Mom hadn't probed the issue further. Nothing good would come from discussing the gory details of the night Mr. Sinclair died. I knew I'd killed Mr. Sinclair, and Mom knew I'd killed him, but that was enough. Mom didn't need to live with what I'd done. I was the one who'd murdered Mr. Sinclair, not her.

CHAPTER 31

I stepped outside the following Saturday evening, about to go for a jog, when I bumped into Gavin.

"What are you doing here?" I asked.

"Your mother around?"

"She's away on another business trip," I shook my head. "Why?"

"Mind if I come inside for a sec?"

"Sure." I unlocked the front door and Gavin trailed in behind me. "What's up?"

"We need to talk."

I locked my arms together. "Hope you aren't angry about Mr. Sinclair."

"Not about that. Not directly, at least."

"Okay."

"You need to drop whatever you've got planned today and go to my beach house."

"That's a long way to go for a random trip," I said.

"It'll be worth it."

"What's going on?"

"If you go to my beach house, then you'll get closure about Liam's death," Gavin said. "Anyone with a brain cell can tell you miss him."

"Closure? What? Why can't you tell me what's going on?"

"I'm not at liberty to tell you more but trust me. It'll be worth the trip."

I pondered for a second. Gavin helping me the night I'd murdered Mr. Sinclair had proved I could trust him. It wasn't like Mr. Sinclair could've been waiting for me at the beach house. He was absolutely, positively dead. And if I could get some healing from whatever was at Gavin's vacation home, then I wouldn't protest. I didn't deserve to be miserable for the rest of my life. Being seventeen meant I still had something like another sixty to seventy years ahead of me. I needed more than fleeting happiness.

"There's something else," Gavin said.

"What?" I asked.

"Don't have sex on my bed if you stay the night," Gavin said. "Liam has been staying the guest bedroom, so you can use that."

"Gavin!" I exclaimed.

"Lighten up. Don't pretend that thought didn't cross your mind."

I knocked on the front door of Gavin's vacation home four times, then Liam whisked me inside before the front door slammed shut.

My breathing slowed. It was Liam. He was alive. He was *alive*.

I remained silent. I believed the mantra about life being stranger than fiction, but I'd never considered Liam could still be breathing. It was like a fairytale. Miracles were only supposed to happen in Disney movies, not real life.

Liam pulled me in for a quick kiss, but I pulled back after a beat.

"Something wrong?" he asked.

"We have to talk, Liam."

"I know."

"Living room couch?" I asked.

"Sure."

"I can't believe it," I said sometime later, adjusting my posture on the faded sofa. "You stockpiled your blood and staged a crime scene to drive your father crazy with guilt in hopes he'd turn himself in to the police for Evelyn's death."

"But you killed him…"

"I won't apologize for that," I said, not even blinking.

"Now you know why I had a mini-fridge in my room."

"How did you even get the vials to stockpile your blood?" I asked.

"Gavin's mother is a nurse at Greenwood Hospital."

"So?"

"He paid his mom a visit one day at work and snuck away for a moment to steal a bunch of test tubes. He was the one who convinced me the plan might be necessary one day, my home situation being what it was and all."

Wow. Liam had an answer for everything. My head wouldn't stop spinning. Life was so much more complicated than it should've been. Liam had gambled a lot with his plan, and I didn't know what I would've done if the scheme backfired on him. More than it had by me killing his father, anyway.

My gaze intensified. "What about hospital security cameras?"

"There weren't any around the area he stole the empty vials from."

"If you trusted Gavin enough, then you should've trusted me," I said.

Liam averted his gaze. "What's done is done."

"How long were you gonna stay here?" I asked.

"The ocean might be too cold for swimming right now, but Gavin's family leaves the place running all year."

Liam had to be kidding. Nobody in their right mind would pretend to be dead indefinitely. If there was no end date for his scheme, he'd just traded one prison for another. His father was dead, but letting people believe he was gone meant he was still only surviving. Not living.

"Unbelievable," I said.

"I get that you're angry…"

"That's not the word I'd use."

"Fine. You're pissed off," Liam said. "And you've got every right to feel that way."

"Your plan to drive someone crazy kind of worked. You just bet on the wrong person."

"I never wanted to hurt you," Liam pleaded.

"You've got a funny way of showing that."

"Where does that leave us?" Liam asked, reaching out tentatively to cover my hand with his own.

He couldn't be serious. Our relationship status was hardly important at the moment. I still hadn't finished processing my feelings about his miraculous resurrection.

"That's the least of my concerns," I said.

"Fair enough."

I stood. "You've gotta decide what you wanna do, because you can either stay dead or return to the living. But you can't have both."

"I know," Liam snapped, face turning a violent shade of red.

"I'm gonna go."

"Don't you wanna stay for dinner? Aren't you happy I'm alive?"

"You can't guilt me into being in a relationship," I said.

"Wasn't trying to. We're free of my father, and we should celebrate."

"Not in the mood." I scurried out of the living room, then slammed the front door behind him before walking down the front steps.

Liam might've been alive, but I hadn't gotten a piece of my heart back. If anything, an additional piece of my heart had been stolen. Liam would've told me about his plan if he loved me. So, we were done for good. I'd tolerated a lot in the past, but I could have no future with a guy who'd let me think he was dead. If Liam was capable of doing something so cruel, then I didn't know him as well I'd thought.

CHAPTER 32

Gavin, Natalie, and Mona sat next to me at one of the tables in front of the high school's main entrance several days after my encounter with Liam. Gray clouds were clustered together in the sky while trees bobbed in the wind and a pile of red, orange, and yellow leaves scattered into the distance.

"Oh my god! Liam is alive?!" Mona exclaimed.

"Not so loud," I hissed.

Gavin looked up from his textbook. "Not sure why you care. Liam told me about your reunion, and to say he was pissed is an understatement."

"Not my job to prop up him up," I said.

Natalie touched my wrist. "You okay?"

"I don't wish bad on Liam or anything. I just can't be with someone who doesn't respect me enough to include me in a plan like this."

Gavin tapped his pencil against the table. "That's harsh."

"How would you feel if Mona did that?" I asked.

"I would never do that to Gavin. Care about him too much." Strands of Mona's hair fluttered in the wind. "But maybe Liam didn't wanna burden you."

"Not his call to make," I said.

"If you wanna blame anyone, you should blame me," Gavin said. "The whole thing was my idea, and it was stupid. I should've come up with another way to help Liam when I saw him covered in bruises the first day of football practice this year."

"Don't make excuses for him," I said.

"He cares about you."

"How did you two even keep in touch after he faked his death?"

"Burner phone."

My attention shifted to Natalie. "You never told me what happened with the essay contest. Did you hear back?"

The topic was too casual, but I still had to ask. Friendship required a joint effort, which meant taking an interest in Natalie's life like she did with me. Plus, I wanted to change the subject.

"Not yet. But thanks for asking," Natalie said.

"You're gonna have to make up your mind about your feelings for Liam," Mona pointed out. "The irony is Liam will be more drawn to you if you push him away."

I shivered, but I wasn't sure if my reaction was because of Mona's comment or the chill filling the air. She was right, whether I enjoyed admitting the truth or not. The minor friction in our relationship might make Liam more attracted to me, and I didn't know what I'd do if I caved. Sex was fleeting, like everything else in life.

"Don't remind me," I said.

Gavin's focus returned to his textbook. "No offense, but you killed his father."

"You aren't supposed to judge me about that," I said.

"Just stating a fact."

"I might've brought the knife with me," I said. "But he was practically goading me, reveling in how miserable I was."

"No need to rehash the past," Mona said.

Thank goodness for Mona. At least she wanted to keep the peace. More than I could say about Gavin. He seemed more intent on lecturing me than giving advice. It made me want to punch a pillow. Gavin would've accepted me without any hesitation if he was really my best friend. Not tried to parent me.

"Give me one good reason I should forgive Liam," I demanded.

"Life is short," Gavin said.

I made a pig-like snort. "You can do better than a silly cliché."

"It's the truth." Gavin unscrewed his water bottle, then took a sip. "Do you really wanna sacrifice your happiness for pride?"

Damn. I couldn't argue with that, no matter how hurt I was by Liam's secrets. Loving and hating someone at the same time was possible, and at some point, I'd probably have another encounter with him.

Liam and I sat on my living room couch several afternoons after the discussion in front of the school.

"Thanks for meeting with me," Liam said.

"Whatever happens should be in person, not over text or by phone."

"Your mom around?"

"She's away on another business trip."

"Oh." Liam placed his hands on his lap. "I'm coming back to school Monday morning. Just thought you should know."

"What about the police?" I asked.

"I told them a version of the truth."

"Meaning?"

"That I stockpiled my blood and staged a crime scene so people would think I was dead," Liam said. "Explained I was afraid of my father."

"And?"

"They accepted it was a prank gone wrong.".

Good for Liam. He of all people deserved something to go right for him after all the bullshit he'd endured.

"What about those charges your father filed?" I asked.

"Remember, silly? He dropped those charges."

I remained silent.

"Where does that leave us?" Liam asked.

"I can't be in a relationship with someone who kept such a big secret from me. It drove me to commit murder."

"I know." Liam held my hands, and I didn't swat them away. "But I'm still in love with you, and the time we spent together means something."

"Believing you've become a better person than you were last May doesn't change the fact that we're toxic to each other. Relationships aren't supposed to be this much work."

He pulled his hands away. "Fine."

"Probably easier to pretend like we don't know each other."

"Okay."

"You aren't angry?" I asked.

"Forcing someone to be in a relationship they don't wanna be in isn't gonna work," Liam said. "But I want you to know one thing. Together or apart, we're gonna get the fresh start we deserve. I'm keeping your secret because you don't deserve to spend the rest of your life in prison because of my father."

Wow. I couldn't help being impressed by Liam's response. He was acting more mature than I would've if the situation were reversed.

"Thanks," I forced out.

Liam clapped my knee, then stood. "Don't have to thank me. Not ratting you out is the right thing to do."

"Can I ask one question?"

"Sure."

"Where are you staying?" I asked.

"At home. I'm working on getting emancipated."

Well, at least Liam had more good news. I couldn't imagine how he would've felt escaping his father only to be trapped by another bad situation. Living on his own might've been just what Liam needed. For some people, being alone was freedom.

"Hope it works out. You deserve happiness," I said.

"Thanks. Anyway, I should go."

"Goodbye, Liam."

"Bye." Liam darted out of the living room and a few seconds later I heard the front door slam behind him.

Waiting until Liam left before crying proved best. Not wanting to reunite with him didn't mean I couldn't grieve our relationship. I couldn't just snap my fingers and forget about our past, no matter how hard I tried. But maybe, just maybe, my heart would ache less someday. Optimism was my only choice—I couldn't be miserable for the rest of my life. If I was, then there wasn't much point to anything.

CHAPTER 33

I exited the school bathroom one morning a few weeks after my official breakup with Liam. I bumped into someone and looked up. It was him.

Liam pressed his hands together. "I wasn't trying to bother you. I've been respecting your boundaries and staying away."

I gave a short laugh. "Don't worry about it. I should've paid attention to where I was going."

Liam looked me over. "Have you been crying?"

"No."

"Your face is all red, and your eyes are puffy."

"Don't worry about it." I tried walking away, but Liam grabbed my hand and led me into an adjacent hallway. This was worse than summer school. The last thing I wanted was to discuss my life since our breakup. We had no reason to talk—the world would survive if we weren't friends. Sometimes, the past was better left in the past.

"What's going on?" he asked.

"Not important."

"Is someone giving you a hard time?"

"Nope. Nothing to do with school."

Liam scanned the hallway—we still had it to ourselves—then he leaned closer. "Something wrong with your mother?"

"I owe you an apology."

"For what?" Liam asked.

"For judging you about faking your death."

"I'm not mad. I can't tell you how to feel."

I let out the longest sigh of my life. "Please let me say what's on my mind."

"Sorry."

"I realized life isn't black and white, and people make mistakes," I said.

"Where is this coming from?"

I inhaled a deep breath. "Doesn't matter. Just wanted to let you know I'm sorry."

"Us not dating anymore doesn't mean I want you to be miserable."

"It's too awful," I said, pulse increasing. Knowing my luck, Liam would get the truth out of me.

He snickered. "Can't be worse than what you did to my father. No offense, or anything."

"It's not."

"Then tell me."

Liam should've won an award for most determined teenager. He was gonna get the truth from me, and there wasn't a damn thing I could do about it. There was something about the look in Liam's eyes that made me think maybe it was because he still cared about me. I almost regretted giving up on our relationship because I'd let my pride get in the way of reconciling.

"I forgot to go to the grocery store a couple of weeks ago," I blurted.

"So?" Liam asked, almost laughing.

"My mother went instead of me and got in a car accident."

Liam rolled up the sleeves of his plaid flannel shirt. "Is she okay?"

"The car accident isn't the issue."

"I don't follow you."

"They ran tests on her at the hospital, and it turns out she has a heart condition."

He clapped his hand over his mouth. "I'm so sorry, Connor."

"She's on a transplant list waiting for a new heart."

"You should've come to me." Liam looked concerned.

Well, the world didn't revolve around him. Even if his intentions were pure in this instance. Being vulnerable with another human was the last thing I wanted after everything that had happened since Dad's death. It didn't matter how much time passed since Dad died. The event was something I'd have to live with. I'd always be that fragile kid who'd lost his father too soon. And now that I wasn't with Liam, I didn't owe him anything besides superficial politeness.

"You aren't my boyfriend, so it's not your job to care about me." I started to walk away when Liam tugged at my sleeve.

"Stop pretending to be brave," he said.

"It's nobody's job to solve my problems."

"Her age must make her a good candidate for a transplant, right?"

I stepped away from Liam, then buried my head in my palms. "She still has to find a heart. God. I don't know what I'd do if my mother died. Losing both parents in less than a year would be…" I had to laugh a little. "Something else."

The warning bell rang, then a few students ran by us.

"I'm having a party Saturday night," Liam said. "You're welcome to come if you wanna blow off steam. You don't even have to speak to me."

Whether or not I accepted Liam's invitation didn't matter. His thoughtfulness was what counted. And his caveat about not having to interact with him had been kind. Some people might not have been so considerate.

I wiped my eyes with my sleeve. "Thanks."

"I don't know how, but your mother is going to be okay."

"If only life were that simple. Although I appreciate the sentiment."

I sat on the floor of the same room I'd occupied during Evelyn's Spring Fling party, sobbing.

The door opened while music from an adjacent room vibrated throughout the second floor, drowning out my sobs. Liam entered the room, holding a cup.

"I'm sorry. I didn't realize you were in here," Liam said.

I choked. "Doesn't matter."

"Have you been crying again?"

"My mom is having her heart surgery today. I just needed some privacy for a phone call."

"That's great they found a donor so quickly." Liam shuffled over to me, sat on the ground, then placed a hand on my back. "Don't you wanna be at the hospital?"

It was nice of Liam to keep me company despite the fact that he was the party's host and should've been tending to his guests. More guilt burned through my insides. I didn't know what the fuck I'd been thinking when I refused to give him a second chance. Liam and I weren't toxic—I never felt unsafe around him. All relationships were complicated. I was just too lazy and hadn't wanted to put in the effort. And I'd have to live with my stupidity for the rest of my life—someone should've smacked me for letting the best thing that had ever happened to me walk away.

"Maybe later," I said.

"Okay. Cool."

Liam and I held eye contact for a long time before I kissed him. He didn't push me away, and his palms caressed my cheeks. He even gave me a little tongue.

"Sorry. I don't mean to lead you on," I said after pulling back from the kiss a couple of minutes later.

"I'm emancipated now. I can look after myself,—I wouldn't have kissed you if I didn't want to."

"You're emancipated? That's great!" I said.

"I wanna ask you a question, and I need an honest answer."

"Sure."

"Did you kiss me because you were scared about your mother, or because you wanted to make out?"

I didn't wince. "Second one."

It was true. Nothing—whether a situation or a person—made me do anything I didn't wanna do. If anything, Mom's medical problem had given me the push to do whatever I wanted. Kind of like how being drunk didn't change magically change people's personalities. Just gave people the confidence to do what they couldn't sober.

He smirked. "Okay. Good to know."

"What do you wanna do?" I asked.

Liam couldn't keep his eyes off me. "I had one idea, but it's up to you. I don't wanna pressure you to do anything you don't want to."

I could infer where this conversation was going, but it would've been nice if Liam could spell out his intentions in concrete terms. Ambiguity often just complicated life, even if a lot was said with what wasn't said.

"I'm fine with whatever you have in mind."

"Cool." Liam wiggled his eyebrows. "Not like we haven't done this thing before. It'll be like a trip to Starbucks."

CHAPTER 34

I sat on the wooden bench in the park on Main Street several afternoons after attending Liam's party. Sunlight poked through the cloudy sky, although the wind hadn't stopped blowing enough to let the sun warm things up.

Liam approached the bench. "Thanks for meeting me."

"No problem."

He sat next to me.

"My mother survived the surgery, and the doctors are optimistic about her recovery," I said. "But I'm sure you didn't call me here to talk about that."

"I'm glad your mother is doing okay. But you're right. I didn't call you here for an update on her condition."

"What's up?" I asked.

"The other night was fun," Liam blurted.

A woman in the distance hollered at a girl standing by a food truck. The girl darted towards the woman.

My mind couldn't help replaying what had happened that night in Liam's guest bedroom. Life encompassed a series of moments—both big and small—and my encounter with Liam at his party had been a huge one.

Liam rolled off me, then lay on his back before tucking his right hand under the side of his head. He had a cheesy grin on his face. "That was something. Almost like nothing's changed between us," he said.

"Yeah," I mumbled.

Liam stroked my hair. "Hope you don't regret what happened."

"I don't."

"Neither do I." Liam's cheeks flushed. "No pressure, but you're welcome to stay the night if you don't wanna be alone."

"Thanks."

Cawing birds snapped me out of the memory. I kept my eyes averted from Liam's. I didn't know how I was supposed to make eye contact with the ex I'd had sex with a couple of days ago.

"You don't have to be embarrassed about what happened."

"You're the one who wanted to meet with me."

"A guy asked me out, but I told him I needed time to sort things out," Liam said. "I know you wanted to break up because of everything that happened, but I wanted to give you one last chance in case you changed your mind."

"Liam, please!"

"You don't have to make a decision now," he continued. "But if you wanna get back together, then meet me here Thursday afternoon at 3:00 P.M."

My blood pumped through my body faster. There could be no more sitting on the sidelines. I had a choice to make. Unfortunately, my decision wasn't that simple. Wanting a second chance with Liam couldn't mean forgetting about Mom's issues. This might not have been the right time to reform a relationship. But if I didn't reunite with Liam, I'd have to live with possibly losing him forever. I might've been about to get the biggest headache of my life.

"Thanks for giving me a little time," I said.

"Of course."

I remained silent.

"And I want you to know you can come to me if you ever need anything because of your mom," Liam said. "Doesn't matter if we're together or not. Nobody should have to go through what you're dealing with alone."

"Thanks."

Gavin pulled me aside the following morning in the school hallway.

"Did I do something wrong?" I asked.

Gavin shook his head. "Wanted to make sure you're doing okay with what's going on with your mom's health."

"I'm coping."

"What about Liam?" he asked.

"I've gotta decide if I wanna take him back."

"How long do you have to make a decision?"

"Until tomorrow at 3:00 P.M."

"I'm gonna say something to you, but it's only because we're friends, so please don't get mad at me if you hate my advice."

I nodded. "Okay."

"Don't let your mom's medical crisis stand in the way of your happiness," Gavin said. "You and Liam might only be seventeen, but it'd be a shame to waste that connection if you can sort through your issues."

Creepy. It was if Gavin had read my mind. His comment was along the same lines as my thoughts yesterday.

"If you can forgive me for my role in Liam's 'death,' then you should forgive Liam," Gavin said. "No offense or anything."

"It's not that."

He shot me an inquisitive look. "Then what?"

A couple of tears rolled down my face. "I'm tired of being scared and vulnerable. This feeling of my entire life imploding on a moment's notice isn't fun."

"It's called being human."

I glared at him.

"But the feeling will pass. Promise," Gavin continued.

I walked through the park the following afternoon, discovering Liam waiting for me on the park bench we'd sat at the other day. He smiled at me before he stood.

"You came?" he asked.

"Don't tell me you had doubts."

"Just nerves. What changed your mind?" he asked.

"I'm tired of being miserable and alone."

"Wow."

I chuckled. "But you've gotta promise me one thing."

"Anything."

"Never let me think you're dead again. No matter how good your intentions are."

"I can live with that," Liam said.

"Losing you almost killed me."

"I know…"

"Hopefully, the guy who asked you out won't be too disappointed."

"Fuck him. He doesn't matter." Liam pulled me against his body, and his lips brushed against mine while the wind whipped through the air. His hands traveled to my cheeks, tracing the contours of my skin.

Reuniting with Liam was the right choice. I needed to grow up. Relationships didn't exist in a vacuum or bubble in real life like they did in television shows and movies. But I wouldn't fret in light of that fact. Mr. Sinclair had been our biggest obstacle, and he was dead. That was the only thing that mattered.

I stood in front of my bedroom mirror the following weekend adjusting my hot pink tie, which matched my blazer and shorts.

Someone knocked on my bedroom door.

"Come in," I said.

The door opened, revealing Liam. He walked over to me, then adjusted my tie from behind.

"Figures you'd take the longest to get ready," Liam said.

I smirked. "Whatever."

Liam didn't respond. Instead, he hummed.

"We need to laugh about some things no matter how awful they might be," I said. "But if you'd prefer, I don't say stuff like that, then tell me. I'm not psychic."

"You're fine."

"Then what's the problem?" I asked.

"I was thinking about my mother. She taught me how to tie a tie because my father couldn't be fucking bothered."

I squeezed his hand. "Sorry."

"Don't be. I got the last laugh.".

Our friends ran into my bedroom.

"You aren't supposed to have sex 'til after the Winter Dance is over," Gavin said.

"Gavin!" I exclaimed.

He might've meant well, but he needed to cool it with the sex comments. Not everyone was horny 24/7/365. Some people—like me—actually considered other things. Sex was only one experience out of the many I hoped to go through in life.

Mona patted my back. "Lighten up."

"Liam was helping me with my tie—not that it's any of your business," I said.

Jordon rolled his eyes. "Sure."

"Do I look like I know how to tie a tie?" I asked.

"He has a point," Evan backed me up.

Violet eyed me. "The outfit looks great."

I nodded. "Thanks."

"We should take a photo. We're gonna want this moment to last forever." Natalie ran her fingers through her hair.

She had a point. We deserved to remember the good times, too. Our lives were more than covering up a murder.

"Good idea," Mona piped up. "As much as I hate to say that after how much you've boasted about winning that damn essay competition."

"Let her have a little fun," Violet poked Mona.

We all huddled together before Natalie raised her iPhone. The phone's camera flashed as she snapped the photo. She passed her iPhone around, and none of us had any complaints about the group selfie.

A warm feeling spread through my body as we rushed out of my bedroom. For the first time in a long time, I was happy. I was building a life for myself—both with Liam as my boyfriend and with Natalie, Mona, Gavin, Violet, Evan, and Jordon as my friends—and nobody could steal that from me.

Mr. Sinclair had been a piece of shit, yet he'd taught me a lesson— the importance of standing up for myself. I was no longer that scared boy lying in Liam's bed, wondering if Mr. Sinclair would break down the locked door. I was someone who would protect my happiness at all costs.

We all piled into the limo, and Liam gave me a look that meant I needed to get with the program.

Yeah. My life would be just fine.

Chris Bedell's previous publishing credits include Thought Catalog, Entropy Magazine, Chicago Literati, and Foliate Oak Literary Magazine, among others. His debut YA Fantasy novel IN THE NAME OF MAGIC was published by NineStar Press in 2018. His 2019 books include his NA Thriller BURNING BRIDGES (BLKDOG Publishing) and his YA Paranormal Romance novel DEATHLY DESIRES (Deep Hearts YA). In addition to his YA Thriller BETWEEN LOVE AND MURDER, Chris has another book releasing in 2020. His YA Contemporary I'LL SEE YOU AGAIN (Deep Hearts YA). Furthermore, Chris graduated with a BA in Creative Writing from Fairleigh Dickinson University in 2016.